THE TOFF
AND OLD HARRY

The Toff and Old Harry

JOHN CREASEY

WALKER AND COMPANY New York

Author's Note. The character of Snub Higginbottom appears in only a few of the Toff books written about this period, and makes one re-appearance in a later story—*Vote For the Toff.*

First published in the United States of America in 1970 by the Walker Publishing Company, Inc.

Published simultaneously in Canada by The Ryerson Press, Toronto.

Library of Congress Catalog Card Number: 73-126117

Printed in the United States of America from type set in the United Kingdom.

ISBN: 0-8027-5217-9

CONTENTS

CHAPTER I

SMALL FORTUNE

"IT isn't any use saying that I shouldn't have got myself into this mess," said George Armitage. "I'm in it, and I've got to get out of it somehow." His blue eyes were bloodshot, his brown hair tousled, his young face taut with anxiety. "You could easily afford to——"

"My dear George," interrupted Philip Rowse, "you need a small fortune. I haven't a lot of money to throw away."

"You throw it away on your fancy women!" flared George. "Why, you simply ooze money. Look at this flat!" He waved his arms wildly about the large, luxuriously furnished room.

"I think you'd better go," said Rowse. "I've got you out of too many scrapes already; it's time you stood on your own feet. And, George—don't make any more cracks about my friends, or I'll throw you out."

"I'd like to see you try!" cried George. "Come on—try to throw me out. You're nothing but a fool with money; anyone with a pretty face and a good figure can squeeze it out of you. But when I come along and ask for a trifle, you fling insults in my face. Come on, throw me out!"

Rowse looked at George Armitage distastefully. Rowse was tall and dark, handsome in a sleek, sallow fashion, dressed like a fashion-plate in the *Tailor and Cutter*. A myriad of tiny lines at the corners of his brown eyes gave him a dissipated look, somehow belied by his good complexion.

"I don't intend to brawl with you," he said. "Better go and sleep it off."

"So you're scared," sneered George, taking a step forward. "That's just like you—you smug, self-satisfied,

7

conceited, bragging swine. If it weren't for you I shouldn't be in this mess; it's all your fault."

"If you would blame yourself for a change, you might get somewhere," said Rowse. "I've said my last word, George. Out you go."

Rowse moved forward. George struck out, but Rowse caught his right wrist and twisted it, forcing a gasp of pain from him. Almost in the same movement Rowse swung him round. Had the door been open he would have hustled him straight into the hall, but he had to pause and fumble for the handle with his left hand. George was so astounded that he didn't resist; anyhow, the pain in his arm was paralysing. Then the door opened from the outside, making Rowse pause and George gape.

A girl stood on the threshold; a tall, slim vision.

"Anne!" exclaimed Rowse. "What are you doing here?" He thrust George away, and George staggered into a chair. "My dear, I didn't expect you for another half-hour," Rowse went on.

"Apparently not," said the girl dryly. She glanced at George, then back at Rowse. "Aren't you being rather rough?"

"No rougher than that young fool deserves," said Rowse.

"Oh," said Anne. "He looks rather upset."

Her calmness was part of her attractiveness—something which greatly impressed George, in spite of his discomfiture. Her eyes were the blue of cornflowers, her hair the colour of ripe corn. She was well made-up, but not excessively rouged and painted, like most of Rowse's girl friends.

"Never mind whether he's upset," said Rowse in a sharper voice. "George, get out."

"I'm damned if I will!" snapped George with fresh courage. "You know what I've come for. If—if *she* asked for a thousand pounds you'd give it to her like a shot!"

"Really!" said Anne, her eyes widening.

"You know darned well he would!"

"Then there must be unsuspected depths of generosity in

him," said Anne. "Philip and I aren't quite on those terms, are we, Philip?" She smiled. "Does he *owe* you a thousand pounds?" She seemed genuinely curious, still calm and detached, looking at George as if he were a new kind of creature.

"My dear, don't take any notice of him," said Rowse, who had recovered his composure. "He has a curious notion that I set him on the downward path. He lost a packet on horses, and stole to recoup himself. Now he's been given twenty-four hours in which to repay, or be handed over to the police. The mistake was to give him time to pay. Even if he swindled someone of the money, he'd be up to the same tricks before you could say snap."

The girl went to a low, luxurious chair and sat on the arm, leaning forward and looking at George curiously.

"Philip!" George took a step forward, his hands outstretched in supplication, his temper quite gone. "I—I'm sorry if I've behaved like a swine, but you're my last hope. I must get that money. You—you know it *is* partly your fault. Every tip you gave me was a loser. I didn't realize I was plunging so deep, things caught up with me before I'd thought about it. And it—it really wouldn't make any difference to you. A thousand pounds—why, you'd pay it for a picture any day of the week. Look at that!" He pointed to a small oil painting, a lovely landscape, like a window opening on to the English countryside. "You paid four thousand three hundred for that only a month ago, and boasted about it. It's only one of a dozen like it here."

"You're quite wrong," said Rowse. "There isn't another like it in the world. No, George. There are limits to this blood-being-thicker-than-water business."

"You—you mean that?"

"That's my last word."

George muttered: "All right, I won't worry you any more. I won't worry anyone any more." He went slowly towards the open door. "The best thing I can do is throw myself in the river."

"I don't suppose anyone would miss you," said Rowse.

Anne shot him a quick, disapproving glance.

George stiffened and clenched his hands, turned—and then went forward again. A glass bowl on a small, exquisite Regency table quivered and tinkled as he stepped heavily.

"Wasn't that a bit cruel?" Anne asked in a detached voice.

"He deserves it," said Rowse.

"Oh, doubtless," said Anne. "But will you think so if you hear that he's been pulled out of the river?"

"My dear, don't get silly notions like that," said Rowse. "A man who intends to commit suicide never talks about it. The best thing that could happen to that young idiot is a spell of prison life. It would knock some sense into him. Don't ask me to weep crocodile tears over a silly young wastrel. He's run through ten thousand pounds in two years, and if I gave him a thousand he'd go and blue it and still be in trouble. He's had every chance—he even had a flourishing little antique business, but let it go to rack and ruin. Forget him!"

The front door closed.

"What will you have to drink?"

"Nothing, thanks," said Anne. "I'm going to save that young man from committing suicide." She smiled gaily, and moved towards the door.

"Don't waste your time," advised Rowse. "He wants a sharp lesson."

"His death would be on my conscience," said Anne. "I'm not responsible for yours, but mine matters a trifle. I'll soon be able to talk him out of it. *Is* he a relation of yours?"

"A cousin." Rowse tried to take her arm, but she evaded him, stepped into the hall and opened the front door. She closed it in his face.

.   .   .   .   .

George reached the end of Garron Street, in Chelsea, and swung round the corner without looking behind him.

Therefore he did not see Anne—and he did not see the curly-haired young man with a snub nose who was on the opposite corner, eyeing the girl with unconcealed admiration. George swung on towards the Embankment, which was not far away. This was a quiet, secluded part of Chelsea, between King's Road and the river, and few people were about. George's eyes glittered and his hands were clenched tightly; he went so quickly that Anne had difficulty in keeping fairly close behind him.

Had she glanced round she would have seen that the young man with the snub nose was following her.

George reached the roadway. A small string of private cars, cyclists and lorries made him pause on the kerb. Still he didn't look round, but stared across the road towards the flat, rippled surface of the Thames. The river was already reflecting lights from the bridge near by, although this was early dusk on an April evening.

The traffic passed, except one car still approaching.

Anne drew level with George.

"Don't you think——" she began, touching his arm.

George started, glared round, shook himself free and plunged into the road. The car horn hooted urgently, the car swerved towards the pavement and the girl drew back hastily. George hardly noticed the confusion he had caused, but strode on and reached the other pavement.

It looked as if he meant to carry out his threat.

The road was clear for a moment, and the girl hurried across as blindly as George had done. But as she reached the far kerb the young man with the snub nose appeared, as if conjured out of the air. And he took her arm, gripping it gently, and said:

"The time is not yet."

Anne pulled herself free. "What do you mean?"

"Precisely what I say—a novel change in this wicked world of duplicity, isn't it? I mean, he won't do himself in until after dark. Look!" He pointed towards a large and massive figure approaching with a steady, heavy gait.

"There is a policeman. Suicides always wait until the policeman's back is turned and the darkness of night covers their last shame."

George had also seen the policeman.

He leaned against the parapet and took out a cigarette-packet. He looked into it, scowled, crumpled it up savagely, and flung it into the river. But he showed no sign of throwing himself in now, and the policeman plodded past him and took up a position twenty yards away. From there he surveyed the passing traffic and the buildings opposite, and, out of the corner of his eye, the desperate-looking young man.

"You see," said he with the snub nose. "Nothing like a man in blue to put a damper on suicides."

"How do you know what he means to do?" demanded Anne.

"It is given to some to see visions," declared the young man. There was a merry twinkle in his grey eyes and a smile on his full lips. He had curly, fair hair and a healthy complexion, and a lean, lithe body.

"Don't be a fool," said Anne.

"The truth is, I'm a friend of George," said the young man more seriously. "I know that he's being pushed hard and that he turned to his cousin as a kind of last resort. And I thought I'd better keep an eye on him. Leave him to me, will you, honey?"

Anne looked at him doubtfully, curiously.

"Are you sure he'll be all right? I didn't like the way he behaved at—at my friend's flat."

"George always behaves like the central figure of a great melodrama," declared the snub-nosed young man earnestly, "but I'll talk him out of this heroic gesture. Have no fear. Go and tell dear Philip that he need not lie awake, tormented by visions of a bloated corpse floating in London's murky moat. See you again some time, I hope," he added politely, and he touched his forehead, beamed, and left her.

She hadn't mentioned Rowse by name.

The policeman still watched. George stared into the water, which was growing duller now, except near the bridge and beneath the lamps along the Embankment, which reflected on the sluggish surface and twinkled back lazily. The snub-nosed youth joined George and took his elbow—and Anne saw him proffer a cigarette-case.

They lit up.

The policeman moved on.

Feeling that the crisis was over, Anne walked back across the road. Now that the emergency had gone she felt cold—it was chilly and a wind blew off the river. She hurried back to Garron Street, wondering if she had made a fool of herself, and what Philip Rowse would say when she got back.

He'd probably laugh, and say there had never been any danger of George committing suicide. But—she thought there had been real despair and desperation in those blood-shot eyes.

CHAPTER II

NO FRIEND OF GEORGE

GEORGE watched the crumpled cigarette-packet floating. It looked very white against the dark water. One moment it seemed to be drawing rapidly away from him, the next it was brought towards him by the eddies near the parapet. He felt a dull, hopeless despair.

"Good evening," said a voice at his side.

George glanced round sharply.

"Cigarette?" offered the young man, who had a snub nose. He opened a long case, which was filled with fat cigarettes, and almost before George realized that they were being offered he flicked a lighter.

They lit up.

"Chilly," observed Snub.

"Who the devil are you?"

"Just a friend," said the young man.

"I've never seen you before!"

"As a matter of fact, you have," declared the young man, whose eyes had lost their merry twinkle and who now appeared to be in deadly earnest. "You may not remember, but you've seen me several times. That is the power of obsession over observation. You'd be astonished how much you see but don't notice."

"Oh, would you?" growled George.

"Yes, you would," the other assured him. "It's all a matter of training. I've been trained in the right school. I saw an angry man and a most attractive young woman; I presumed they had quarrelled, and I imagined that the man was likely to throw himself into Old Father Thames, and I thought it just wouldn't do."

"Don't be a fool," muttered George. "I don't know her any more than I know you."

"Really?" said the other in a tone of mild disbelief. "I'm surprised. Wrong diagnosis, right prescription—a cigarette and a word in time. How about a drink?"

"Who *are* you?" demanded George.

It was much darker now, for dark clouds had gathered. Headlights from some of the oncoming cars showed clearly; there were lights at countless windows in flats and houses. The policeman was only a vague shape some distance off, and the girl had disappeared. Night yawned over London— but it did not conceal the look of embarrassment on the face of the young man with the snub nose. He glanced right and left, then lowered his voice.

"Higginbottom," he said, and added hastily, "I was born with it."

"With what?"

"My dear chap! The name. How would *you* like it? I'm told that it has nothing to do with anatomy, but that in the far distant days I had an ancestor who lived in a valley at the bottom of the hill, but it's so long ago that most human beings are unaware of it. Friends call me Snub."

George, with the cigarette half-smoked, actually smiled. He was already feeling better, because this young man's inanities had made him think about something other than his own plight.

"You're an odd fish," he remarked.

"Well, odd, maybe," conceded Snub. "Look here, what's all the gloom about? I mean, there *was* gloom, wasn't there? I didn't like the way you glared at the river, as if you were deciding which fish to feed. How about a drink?" he repeated. "I know a nice, cosy little hostelry which will be open by now, or, if you'd prefer one out of the public gaze, I think I could lay my hands on a bottle of Scotch at my rooms. Yes?"

"I don't see why you're interested in me," said George.

"Not in you alone. In the whole human race. For

instance, that girl," went on the man whose friends called
him Snub. "The word of yester-year was peach, wasn't it?
I hope she won't catch a cold. I hope we don't for that
matter, but we shall if we don't get a move on." He urged
George along the Embankment, and George fell into step.
Soon they passed the constable. "Good evening, officer,"
said Snub, and beamed. "Cold, isn't it?"

The constable nodded and said, "Good night, sir."

"Wonderful, our policemen, aren't they?" remarked
Snub. "If only there weren't criminals and careless drivers,
we could put 'em in a museum or send 'em abroad as dollar
earners. Sorry if I babble, but I'm made that way. My
car's just up here," he added, and they crossed the road and
entered a side turning. The shape of a small car showed,
drawn up against the kerb; another shape, that of a man,
stood a little way from it. "Never like parking on the main
streets," Snub added. "I hate police-courts. Ever——"

"Don't!" cried George.

Snub looked surprised and hurt.

"My dear chap! Sorry. You're allergic to them too, are
you? Nothing unusual, but——"

He stopped again, this time because the dark shape
of a man moved forward. The light was enough for
Snub to see features which, even in the politest of circles,
could only have been called ugly. The newcomer was large
too, with powerful shoulders; he had a broken nose and, it
proved, a harsh and rather displeasing voice.

"Armitage, I want a word with you," he said.

George started, stared, and raised his hands in a sudden
wild flare of alarm.

"I say!" bleated Snub.

"You clear aht," said the newcomer heavily. "And tell
your perishing boss that if you 'ang arahnd any more I'll
clip you over the ear." He made a threatening gesture, but
it ended in a grip on George's arm. "Know this fellow?"
he demanded.

George muttered, "No, I just happened——"

" 'Op it, chum," said the man with the broken nose.

"Now, really," protested Snub, "you can't talk to me like that. Do *you* know *this* fellow?" he asked George—but he backed away under the threatening lift of the big man's hand.

George said, "Yes, I know him."

"If he's making a nuisance of himself——"

"Look here, this is my business," said George, his voice becoming shrill. "Leave it to me, will you?"

"That's the ticket," said the big fellow. " 'Op it."

"Oh, well . . ." said Snub, regretfully.

He went to the car, climbed in, and pulled the self-starter. Then he switched on the headlights; a cloud of evil-smelling fumes billowed out of the exhaust-pipe, and with a roar of its noisy engine the two-seater started off. George and his new companion watched it out of sight. Then the big fellow put his hand on George's shoulder, and said:

"Ever seen 'im before?"

"No."

"What did 'e want?"

"I don't know. He asked me to have a drink——"

"Now don't you go drinking wiv strangers," advised the big fellow. "Look, chum, you're in bad, that's what you are. You'll get three years if you're bunged in the dock. Three years is a 'ell've a long time. Old Harry's been very lenient with you, but——"

"If he'll only give me time!"

"You can't get your 'ands on a thousand quid, not if you try from now to Christmas, *and* you know it. But there's a way you might pay off the debt. A little job you can do. You drive a car, don't you?"

"Yes, of course——"

"Done much driving?"

"I've done some racing, but——"

"Okay," said the big man. "There's a certain job you can do. It's easy. Do it well, and you won't 'ave anything more to worry about. Old Harry's a man of 'is word, see?" He grinned in the darkness. "You just do the job and then keep your trap shut, and it's the easiest way I know of clearing orf a debt of a thousand quid. Okay?"

"What is the job?" demanded George.

"You just come along wiv me," said the big man.

. . . . .

The clear sky of the day had gone; dark clouds scudded across the sky, blotting out the stars. A high wind blew across London, smiting street corners with great gusts, howling along narrow alleys, tearing across parks and gardens. It was past midnight. Up here, on the heights of Muswell Hill, George could see the lights of London disappearing, one by one. He could trace some of the main thoroughfares and see cars with sweeping headlights shining upon houses and windows, here and there a late bus, brightly lit. He sat at the wheel of a powerful Lagonda, knowing the district he was in, but not the name of the street or of the house into which the big man, whose name was Baxter, had disappeared. The nose of the car pointed towards the drive gates, and the road was only a few yards away. Two solitary street lamps, some way off, showed the bending branches of the trees farther along the road.

George kept looking over his shoulder.

The front door of the house opened, light streamed out and was then shut off, but not before he had seen three men come out, Baxter among them. Next moment Baxter opened the door and slid into the seat next to George; the other two climbed into the back of the car.

"Turn right out o' the gates," ordered Baxter.

He continued to give directions until they were out of the Muswell Hill district. George did not know this part of London well enough to be sure where he was heading, but twenty minutes or so later they were in an outer suburb, and soon afterwards were moving swiftly along a country road. Not once did Baxter falter in his directions. The Lagonda had a fine turn of speed; the feel of the car under

NO FRIEND OF GEORGE

his control did much to take George's mind off the 'job' he was doing.

He knew that it was criminal. . . .

There were moments when he felt like jamming on the brakes and refusing to drive on, but every time that impulse swept over him he saw the spectre of a trial and prison, and clamped his jaws.

"You can manage wivvout the 'eadlights," Baxter said suddenly. "Then take the next right."

George slowed down. The sidelights seemed very dim when the headlamps were switched off, and he had to go carefully. But he was able to pick out a signpost, and took the next turning to the right. This was a narrow, bumpy road, and he really needed more light. He could just see hedges looming up on either side. The wind howled and whistled, but there was no rain, so the windscreen was clear. He thought he saw the darkness of a copse, and heard the wind roaring through the trees, but couldn't be sure. Soon he saw something white shine out of the hedge on his left.

"Not this gate, the next one," said Baxter.

There was a second white gate, not fifty yards further on. The Lagonda scraped the posts, and Baxter swore at George. He found himself on a drive, and soon he was able to discern the shape of a house against the sky.

"Okay," said Baxter.

George stopped.

Baxter said: "You're going to wait 'ere for us, see? When we come out, start the engine and don't lose no time. The drive bends, and you come out of the other gate. Turn back the way we came, and step on it."

"All—all right," muttered George.

"And switch orf the lights, you ruddy 'alf-wit?" growled Baxter.

The three men left the car, and George sat there in the darkness. He longed to light a cigarette, but was afraid to strike a match. Now and again he shivered, not wholly because of the cold. He knew that he was making an utter fool of himself, but—if this night's wild adventure freed him from danger and anxiety it would be worth it. It seemed ages since he had been easy in his mind. A new idea struck him. This episode might only make his plight worse. There was no guarantee that he wouldn't be compelled to drive Baxter again. If he had any sense he would go off now. Take the car, leave them stranded, that would . . .

But they knew where he lived.

They'd catch him.

A light shone out suddenly in the house from a first-floor window. He saw the moving figure of a woman—and then an arm was raised, holding something that looked like a hammer. The arm fell. The moving figure disappeared, the arm with it. He heard nothing. The silence of the lull made it seem like a dumb-show. Yet it filled him with a wild terror.

The light in the room went out. Soon he heard movements, footsteps. Next moment, Baxter opened the door. One of the other men opened a rear door, flung a case on the seat, and climbed in after it. Soon all three were in the car, and Baxter growled.

"Come on, git moving!"

George started the engine and eased off the brakes. The men were all breathing heavily; one of them kept hissing. That hissing sound got on George's nerves, but he drove along the drive, turned right into the road. Then he heard the men talking behind him, heard them moving about.

"It's not so bad," one said. "More to see than worry about."

"The blood's dripping out," muttered the other, and hissed; he was in pain.

George turned his head.

"You mind yer own," growled Baxter. "We're heading for 'Endon. You just make the West End as quick as you know 'ow, and don't ask no questions."

The car purred along the deserted roads.

The man who had been hurt kept drawing in that hissing breath.

CHAPTER III

REPORT ON A FAILURE

SNUB HIGGINBOTTOM was a miserable man.

He had been charged to follow George, and not to lose him. In the darkened streets of Muswell Hill he had lost his quarry, and so failed on a mission. Being a tenacious young man who disliked failure for its own sake, he behaved in a way which at police-courts is called 'suspiciously' and might, had he not been both careful and elusive, have been charged with 'loitering with intent to commit a felony'. He was searching for the Lagonda in which, he knew, George had driven to this part of London. Some time after midnight, he walked back to his own car, which was in fact no more than a hundred yards from the spot where George had sat waiting for his passengers earlier in the evening.

Nearby was a telephone kiosk.

Snub entered this, put in his four pennies, dialled a Mayfair number and was soon answered by a man who said, as if glumly:

"This is the residence of the Hon. Richard Rollinson."

"Jolly," said Snub, "I've had it. Is he in?"

"Mr. Rollison is out," said the man at the other end of the line.

"I've lost George. Think I'd better come and report in person, or go and watch George's flat?"

"I think you might be well advised to watch the flat," said Jolly. "If Mr. Rollison thinks it unnecessary, I will bring word."

"If he doesn't, bring me a nip of something, will you?" pleaded Snub. "I'm cold, thirsty, hungry and miserable, Jolly." His voice rose. "Hang on," he said sharply, and lowered the receiver.

While he had been speaking a young woman turned the corner and for a few seconds was beneath the light. Snub could hardly believe that he was seeing aright, for it was the girl who had followed George to the Embankment. She glanced quite casually at him. He turned his face away hurriedly and raised the mouthpiece again.

"I've had a break," he crowed. "Rowse's girl friend has just passed. I'll be seeing you!"

He replaced the receiver quickly and stepped into the street. The girl was walking away from him and into the radius of another lighted lamp. Snub slowed down to a brisk walk; it had to be brisk, to keep up with the girl.

He rounded a corner in time to see the girl entering the house. A man had opened the door for her; he could see the fellow's arm.

The door closed.

Snub waited until the hall light had been switched off, then hurried along the drive. He made little sound, because he walked lightly, and on tip-toe. He reached the house and walked to the back; only darkness met him, both downstairs and up. He rubbed the end of his nose, and went round the other side. Standing back from the house was a large garage, and the doors were open.

He saw this in the light which came from a ground-floor room. He crept forward, and, standing close to the wall, peered in at the window.

The girl was standing in front of an overmantel mirror, poking her fingers through her hair. Enticing creature; exciting, too. She turned and smiled at a man who was sitting in an easy chair in front of a dying coal fire. He heard her speak, but could not catch the words. She laughed; to Snub it sounded the merest tinkle.

Then she went forward, and leaned over the man.

Snub craned his neck.

She was kissing the fellow. . . .

Well, no harm in that; he had a white beard and a nearly bald head. He patted the back of her hand, and Snub saw her form the words, 'good night'. Then she went out of the room, and the man picked up a book and began to read.

Snub went into the garage.

First, he closed the doors, then switched on the light. He looked round. It was neat and well-kept. A brand-new tyre hung over a bracket on the wall, with two inner tubes, one of them patched. The shelves were filled with oil-cans, lubricating grease, anti-freeze, a hundred and one oddments. He made a note of the size of the tyre, actually writing it in his diary, and then poked about. Against one wall was a woman's bicycle, fairly new, but that did not help him in his quest. He searched for anything which bore the name 'Lagonda', but there was nothing there. Disconsolate, he switched off the light and went out and walked along the drive—and kicked against something which slithered over the gravel: a paper-covered book. He took it back to the garage, stepping inside and closing the door before putting on the light.

It was a Lagonda service-book.

"*Now* we're getting somewhere!" he exclaimed aloud.

He slipped it into his pocket, switched off the light, and pushed open one of the double doors.

"Good evening," said the girl, who was standing just outside.

.   .   .   .   .

Snub jumped so violently that he nearly fell backwards and before he had recovered the girl had stepped to the wall and switched the light on again. There was no time to dodge past her before she saw him, and the gleam of recognition in her eyes was unmistakable.

"Hallo," said Snub in a subdued voice. "Not my night out."

"I should say it is your night out," said the girl dryly. "What are you doing here?"

"Snooping," said Snub with engaging frankness.

"Yes, I know that. Why?"

"Looking for a jemmy," declared Snub, recovering his wits rapidly.

"A—*jemmy*?"

"Just a little tool," burbled Snub. "A small, iron bar, sharpened at one end, or rather flattened, like a large screwdriver or a small crowbar. Useful for forcing windows and doors and things. People *never* seem to keep a jemmy handy."

"There is a policeman handy," she said.

"Eh? Oh, a Robert. Yes, they're always about when they're least wanted," said Smith. He beamed at her. "George hated the sight of that fellow this evening, but there he was. Poor chap couldn't even throw himself into the river without the police interfering. You never know where they'll pop up next. However—you aren't seriously suggesting that this policeman and I should become better acquainted, are you?"

"That is exactly what I am doing," said the girl. "He's at the end of the road now. Listen."

Snub listened.

Plodding footsteps reached his ears.

"Unmistakable," agreed Snub. "You can tell 'em a mile off."

"Possibly he'll have a jemmy," suggested the girl.

Snub put his head on one side and looked at her steadily. She wasn't smiling, but there was a gleam in her eyes which relieved and assured him. Her hair was ruffled and she had on a loose-fitting coat, which she hadn't worn when she had arrived at the house. He had no doubt that she had either noticed him at the window, or when she had gone upstairs had seen him enter the garage. But if she had really wanted to hand him over to the police she would surely have gone for the constable first, and not met him here.

The plodding footsteps drew nearer and became louder.

"Would you like to ask him?" she inquired.

"Frankly, no," confessed Snub. "I never get on well with policemen after midnight. Look here," he went on hopefully, "shall we stop fencing? I didn't come to steal——"

"I want to know why you did come," said the girl.

"Well——"

"I could scream to attract attention," she said. "And I can describe you perfectly, so there isn't any point in running away. There can't be so many men with noses like yours in London, can there?"

"Hang it, don't blame me for that!" protested Snub, but there was a laugh in his voice. "All right, I'll tell you. I am a friend of George Armitage's, and I think he's having a raw deal. So——"

"I don't believe you're a friend of his," the girl argued. "He didn't seem to know you on the Embankment."

"You don't have to believe me," Snub said reproachfully.

"And even if you were his friend, that wouldn't explain why you're here," she went on. "Don't you think you'd better come inside and tell me all about it?"

The policeman's footsteps were very near now.

"Or shall I——" she began.

Snub said: "Young woman, you aren't as bright as you think you are, and I'm not scared of policemen. Whether I'm a friend of George or not, he's having a raw deal. The simple truth about tonight's escapade is that he gave me the slip, and I think he was lured away by a tough gentleman, who eventually brought him here."

"Nonsense!"

"George came here, at the wheel of your Lagonda."

"Then he was very clever," said the girl. "We haven't a Lagonda."

She did not sound as if she were lying.

"We have an Austin," the girl went on. "It's at the garage having a rebore." She paused, and the policeman's footsteps sounded much further away now. She seemed to lose something of her confidence, although she did not move away from the spot. "Will you please explain why you came here, and why you've told me these lies?" Snub didn't answer, and she went on, "Of course, if you force me to tell the police——"

"That's it," said Snub, suddenly bright. "I'm forcing you to tell the police. I'm asking you to scream for help." He opened his mouth and threw back his head, and the girl momentarily lost her poise; she looked angry. "There you are, you see," went on Snub. "No shout. Of course, it may be sheer coincidence that you live here and George happened along, but I don't think that's very likely. I don't think you want the police on the spot any more than I do. I don't know what you're up to, Esmerelda, but I warn you—have a care. George is keeping nasty company, and not all of your friends are what they might be."

"I'm the best judge of that," said the girl sharply.

"I doubt it. However—if you still insist that it's a coincidence, and you really want to know what I'm doing, meet me at Cherry's for lunch tomorrow."

"I insist——"

"Sorry," said Snub. "I'm in a hurry. Good night!"

He swung away into the garden, out of the light. The girl took a step after him, but stopped. She heard his footsteps on the gravel of the drive. She stood quite still, her face grave, her eyes troubled. Then she switched off the light and went slowly back to the house, using the kitchen door.

CHAPTER IV

CHERRY'S

CHERRY'S was famous. The food was a dream, the cellar a connoisseur's idyll, and there were at least three dishes obtainable at Cherry's and nowhere else in the wide, wide world.

The uninitiated, visiting the restaurant for the first time, would undoubtedly have been disappointed. It looked almost drab, certainly shabby. There were no bright lights, no rococo furniture, no gay furnishings; just comfortable chairs, many of them upholstered with red plush, a scintillating and colourful bar so tiny that a dozen people in it made a crowd, numerous doors, and walls panelled halfway to the ceiling. Above this dark-oak panelling hung pictures of no great merit. A few interesting eighteenth-century prints, some sporting pictures and, over the fireplace in the largest room, a single oil painting of a bunch of cherries—just that. Yet rumour had it that the cherries had been painted by a Royal Academician, as payment for a meal which, in a moment of extravagance, he had declared could only be paid for by art—and from one artist to another.

Cherry himself did not often appear in the restaurant, but stayed in his tiny little office and watched his patrons through a small glass window. Occasionally, when a distinguished—which meant a favoured—patron appeared, Cherry would leave his cubby-hole and go forward, greeting the man—or, more seldom, woman—as a friend would greet a friend. He was content to leave the restaurant in the hands of the incomparable Maurice, who had the manners of a Tsarist Grand Duke and origins in a Montmartre back street.

On the day following Snub's invitation to the girl, Cherry had a visitor in the cubby-hole. It was as well that the visitor, like Cherry, was a small man. He was a Midland manufacturer, who, of all things, contrived also to be an epicure and a gourmet, and Cherry had a profound respect for his judgment of wines.

They were discussing the sad sourness of some recent 'vintage' champagnes when the door was opened—cautiously, or it would have banged Cherry on the back of the head—and Maurice stuck his tiny imperial beard into the room.

"*M'sieu*," he whispered.

"Yes, Maurice?" Cherry, who had a soft, husky voice, used the French pronunciation.

"M'sieur Roll'son," said Maurice simply.

"You are sure?" Cherry jumped up, to the little Midlander's surprise.

"*Mais oui, m'sieu.*"

"I will come," declared Cherry.

He stood up, his brown eyes flashing, rubbing his pink, plump hands together. He gazed at his companion, smiling with almost fatuous satisfaction.

"Now what's all this?" asked the Midlander.

"Mr. Harvey, you have come on an auspicious day," declared Cherry. "It is a long time since Mr. Rollison visited us here. I even began to think that something had, perhaps, displeased him." He gave a little Gallic gesture, although he was English born and bred, despite his acquired foreign way of speaking. "There is hardly a man in London I would rather see than Mr. Rollison. You know him, of course?"

"I can't say I do," said Harvey.

"You do not know—oh, my friend, that is the disadvantage of living in the country," said Cherry, with complete disregard of the urban areas of the Midlands. "Everyone knows Mr. Rollison. He is the great detective."

"Detective!" said Harvey, and laughed.

"Don't misunderstand me," said Cherry. "He is not a policeman. There are times when he makes the police very angry, I am told. But he does not care a fig for them—why should he? Mr. Harvey, there are parts of London where he is more feared than the police."

Harvey sniffed.

"I don't believe it," he declared, and patted his chunky, red face with a silk handkerchief, for it was warm in there.

"As you please," said Cherry rather stiffly. "It is, however, true. And I should perhaps say that the police regard him with favour sometimes—he has a great friend at Scotland Yard. I, Cherry, *know* that he is brilliant, because——"

"All right, then, let's have the story," said Harvey.

Cherry said slowly: "Mr. Harvey, it is a long story, and one day perhaps I shall tell you all of it. Today—there isn't time. But a friend of mine, a very close friend, was in grave danger of being hanged for a murder which another committed, and to this day I believe he would have been hanged had not Mr. Rollison worked for him. And Mr. Rollison did so because I asked him. It seemed so ordinary, just the murder of another girl, but the Toff——"

He raised his hands in another Gallic gesture.

"The who?" demanded Harvey.

"The *Toff*," repeated Cherry; "some people call him that. And in every way he is a toff!"

"I'd like to see this paragon," said Harvey.

"A moment, please," said Cherry.

He stooped down and peered through the hatch. Then he beckoned Harvey, who had to sit down before he could see the corner of the restaurant to which Cherry pointed. There, at a small table, talking to Maurice, was a man at whom most people would have glanced twice, for he was strikingly good-looking. His cheeks were tanned, although it was only spring, and his eyes gleamed; he talked freely to Maurice, who answered so quickly that it was obvious that he was using his native language.

.   .   .   .   .

Having inquired about Maurice's wife, his daughter with
the weak chest, his other daughter with the young man, the
young man himself and Maurice's relatives in France, including his mother in Marseilles, Rollison selected a Chablis, and Maurice went off to fetch it. His place was almost
immediately taken by Cherry. The by-play at the hatch had
not been unobserved, but Rollison greeted Cherry with the
warmth of an old friend, and declared that it was a long
time since he had seen him. He had been out of London.
Ah! Cherry breathed. He and Rollison went through most
of the matters already discussed with Maurice, except that
it was a different set of relatives, including a somewhat dis-
solute son, and they had almost exhausted the conversation
when a girl came into the restaurant.

She was dressed in a smart, black two-piece suit which
would have made most fashionable women feel dowdy; she
was *chic* to the last wisp of her corn-coloured hair.

Rollison stood up, and Cherry heard Rollison murmur,
"And this from Muswell Hill!" He did not explain that
obscure remark, but approached the girl smilingly.

"Good morning," he greeted.

She looked at him coldly.

"I'm sorry I haven't a button nose," said Rollison. "But
I'm afraid I shall have to do. Snub's had to cut the date—
to his eternal sorrow," he added, and smiled at her with
such gaiety that she was taken aback. "Come and sit
down."

"Are you from . . .?" began the girl, then realized the
pointlessness of such a question, and obediently went with
him.

A waiter pulled out her chair, Cherry bowed, the Chablis
arrived; there was a short, breathless pause while Rollison
tasted the wine before he nodded approval. Then suddenly
Rollison and the girl were alone at the table; and although
there were dozens of people in the room, it seemed to the
girl that there was no one here but the two of them.

There was some curious quality about this man. It

wasn't only his smile, or his looks, or his poise; it was a
combination of all three, and drove all other considera-
tions away. There was a gleam in his eyes, a hint of laughter, a touch of dare-devilry. It suddenly occurred to the
girl—as she afterwards admitted—that here was a man living centuries too late; he belonged to an era of gallants long
departed.

"You blunted Snub's descriptive powers," murmured
Rollison, "he did you far less than justice. Your name is
Anne Meriton, you are a friend of Philip Rowse, who has a
cousin named George, and I'm not a friend of George, although I am most interested in him."

"Why? Who are you?"

"My name is Rollison," said Rollison. "There are people
who call me something else, but they hardly count. And I'm
interested in George because, as Snub told you last night,
I think he's going to have a raw deal."

"But if you don't know him——"

"I know some of his friends. Miss Meriton, does any one
of your friends own a Lagonda?"

She did not answer at once, but returned his gaze coolly,
although she looked a little pale. Maurice brought a *con-
sommé*, and she picked up her spoon, hardly realizing that
Rollison had ordered the meal without consulting her.

"Why are you so interested in Lagondas?" she asked at
last. "I haven't one, nor has my uncle, and there's never
been a Lagonda in our garage."

"A neat evasion," said Rollison. "Which of your friends
owns one, Miss Meriton?"

Again she didn't answer.

Their soup-plates were whisked away.

"You know, the world's divided roughly into three parts,"
said Rollison, with the air of a man about to make a brilliant
sally. "The very good, the very bad and the indifferent.
The vast majority of people are indifferent, but George is
unlucky. He's mixed with the very bad, and they have not
improved him. You saw him yesterday on the point of

suicide, didn't you? He was largely to blame, because he's been very silly, but he's quite young——"

"He's old enough to know the difference between right and wrong," said Anne sharply.

"Ah, yes," said Rollison; he seemed to be laughing at her. "But his senses were blunted, like Snub's powers of description! He was just old enough to get put into uniform in the Cyprus troubles, and he saw some fierce action. In the course of that action he did some brave things, and he also saved the life of a close relative of mine. This relative, having seen what George is doing now, asked me if I could help. I'm trying to. George, you see, was invalided out of the Army; recovered, and came into a fortune. That was when he fell in with the wrong people, and they've made a wreck of him, but he's not too old to be repaired. However— George isn't my main consideration——"

He broke off; Maurice appeared, with tender roast duck, green peas, *sauté* potatoes—a dream meal. They began to eat. . . .

"George might be the pivot on which some very odd business will turn," Rollison went on. "He doesn't own a Lagonda, but he was seen driving one late last evening, and he was near your house."

"Is that *so* remarkable?" demanded Anne.

"I'm afraid it might be," said Rollison, and asked casually. "Have you seen the *Evening Cry*?"

"No, I haven't seen a late paper; but what has that to do with it?"

Without answering, Rollison drew a copy of the *Evening Cry* from inside his coat. It was almost sleight-of-hand, as the paper, the right way up, was thrust in front of her eyes. There was a picture of a young woman, another of a safe, broken open, and the main headline read:

GIRL BRUTALLY MURDERED IN ROBBERY

During the night, thieves, interrupted at the country home of Mr. Dwight Evans, brutally murdered Jasmine

Kaye, a maid, by striking her savagely with a hammer or other blunt instrument. A pearl necklace and other valuable jewellery was stolen from the safe.

Anne looked up from the paper, her face pale.
"What are you trying to tell me?" she demanded.
"Read on," said Rollison, "the third paragraph."
She read:

A Lagonda car, with four men in it, was seen in the nearby village of Brayling, a little time after the discovery of the crime, and the police are anxious to interview the driver of the car and his passengers.

"*Have* you a friend who owns a Lagonda?" asked Rollison gently.

CHAPTER V

THE MAN WITH THE LAGONDA

MAURICE hovered and would have approached, but for a slight motion of Rollison's hand. Cherry came from the cubby-hole again, with the red and chunky-faced Midlander and made a bee-line for the couple, then stopped and whispered something into his companion's ear and retreated. All this was done while Rollison looked into Anne Meriton's eyes and gave no sign that he was aware of anything else that was happening in the restaurant.

Anne looked at him searchingly. The pause was long before she said: "Yes, I have."

"Who is it?" asked Rollison.

"I don't think I should tell you," said Anne. "The fact that a friend of mine owns a Lagonda doesn't mean that he had anything to do with—with the murder."

"Of course it doesn't," agreed Rollison. "And as for my right—well, if you mean in the same way as the police have the right to question you, I've none. On the other hand, some people might think it better to tell me than to tell the police."

"There's no reason why the police should question me," said Anne, flushing. "I'm not going to be frightened by anything you say."

"I'm quite sure of that," said Rollison. "Frightened, but not by me. Frightened, or you wouldn't have let Snub go last night; you would have carried out your threat to call the policeman. Frightened, or you wouldn't have come here. I don't like seeing young women as scared as you are, Miss Meriton."

"You're talking nonsense!" flashed Anne, but the flush had gone; she was pale now. That made her eyes bright and

34

her face more striking; even Maurice found it difficult to look away from her.

"All right," said Rollison. "You say you're not frightened, and I'll assume that it's true. So let's say you're very curious. Curious enough to go after George when he left Philip Rowse's flat——"

"I was afraid he would try to kill himself!"

"Ah," murmured Rollison. "You were frightened!" He raised his hand and beamed at Maurice, who now brought coffee-cups and a little brown coffee-pot and whispered, "Liqueurs?" Anne shook her head. "No, thanks," said Rollison, and Maurice faded away.

"I suppose you think you're clever," said Anne.

"Oh no," Rollison assured her. "I'm like you—very curious. George Armitage and Philip Rowse presumably had a quarrel, and you were afraid that George would go straight out and kill himself, and hurried after him to make sure he didn't. I can't understand why you felt so sure."

"It's no business of yours," said Anne. "*I* can't understand what your friend Snub was doing in Garron Street, or why he was watching the flat—he was, wasn't he?"

"Yes, but only incidentally. He was really watching George, because we're interested in these friends of George who aren't doing him any good." Rollison assured her. "We know that George has been badly worried lately over some debt or other, although we can't discover how he got into debt, or why he should be so scared. We wanted to find out. Since Snub followed him as far as Garron Street, we've discovered that Philip Rowse is his cousin, a wealthy man, connoisseur of pictures and fine art, presumably one who could have settled George's troubles by signing a cheque. But he wouldn't do it. Just what happened between them, Miss Meriton?"

"Why *are* you so curious?" she demanded.

Rollison proffered cigarettes from a gold case, and flicked a lighter. He looked at her levelly through the cloud of smoke, and said very gently: "Because I'm afraid that George might be hanged for a murder he didn't commit."

"Oh, you're absurd!"

"Possibly," said Rollison; "but I'm still afraid of it, and I want to prevent it if I can. You see, George will almost certainly be suspected of the murder." He tapped the *Evening Cry* with his forefinger. "And when that happens, the police will check on his recent movements. They'll find out, without much difficulty, that he appealed to his cousin for help; they'll question Rowse, and eventually they'll get round to the fact that you were at the flat when Rowse and George quarrelled. And they might bridge the gap between that and the fact that you've a friend who owns a Lagonda. You would be astonished if you knew how deeply the police inquire when they're on a murder investigation. The things which you and I might think are irrelevant all get a close scrutiny. In this case, I think it's likely that the police will know that George was one of several men—at least three were concerned in that robbery. The girl was able to tell her employer that before she died. A bad business," he added, going off at a tangent. "I've seen a photograph of the back of her head."

"Don't!"

"Oh, I'm sorry," said Rollison, as if he meant it. "What I want you to understand is that the police will almost certainly question you before their inquiries are done, and they may think that by going after George you showed a much deeper personal interest in him than might have been expected from a stranger. So they'll wonder if you and George *are* really strangers. And they'll be looking for his accomplices."

"Are you suggesting that *I* know anything about it?"

"I'm not. The police might."

She didn't speak, but picked up her handbag, put it down again and pulled on her gloves, then got up, took the bag and went out without nodding to him, without glancing round. The doorman opened the door and bowed, and wished her good day, but she didn't answer. She went into the street and turned towards Shaftesbury Avenue, walking quickly, almost blindly.

. . . . .

Cherry allowed a few minutes to pass, saw that Rollison was not yet ready to leave, for he ordered a liqueur, and took the Midlander out to meet him. They were soon lost in a discussion, which became almost heated, on the respective merits of Benedictine and Chartreuse.

. . . . .

Anne Meriton reached Piccadilly Circus, and looked round—not for any special reason, unless it were to see whether Rollison was following her. She was almost disappointed when she saw no sign of him. She did see a heavily built man, wearing a noticeably new Homburg hat, just behind her. He looked blankly past her. She turned down Piccadilly, crossed the road and entered Green Park. It was cold and cloudy and there were few people in the park. Anne walked quickly towards Hyde Park Corner. It wasn't until she was near the park gates that she turned round suddenly, for a dog yapped angrily and a child cried out in alarm.

She saw the man with the Homburg hat.

That was the first time that she suspected the truth about him—that he was a detective. She tried to dismiss the thought as absurd. Rollison had deliberately tried to frighten her by putting the idea into her head. She felt that she disliked Rollison intensely, but it was more than that. His calm manner, all that he had said, had a disturbing quality. She knew that he had been serious, not fooling her.

She crossed to Hyde Park.

The man in the Homburg hat still followed her.

She began to think less about Rollison and more about George.

. . . . .

George was having a bad time.

He had reached his flat in Pelham Mews, near Oxford Street, just after three o'clock in the morning, but that wasn't an unusual time for him to get home. He had made himself some coffee and drunk it black, but hadn't been able to rid himself of the haunting fear about what had happened during the night.

After getting back to the West End he had parked the Lagonda, on Baxter's instructions, in a side street. Baxter had told him simply to go home, keep his mouth shut, and forget about it. Then he and the other two men had slipped away into the darkness.

Forget!

George kept seeing the woman's figure, and the upraised arm, and the hammer. . . .

His was a tiny flat. There was one large room, a small one in which there was just space enough for a single bed and a dressing-table, a tiny bathroom, and a box-like kitchen. He had flung himself down on the bed, fully dressed except for his shoes and his collar and tie, and lain for a long time in the darkness, until at last he had fallen into a restless sleep. He'd awakened, just after eleven o'clock, with a splitting headache and an all-pervading sense of fear.

He made himself more coffee and some toast.

At midday, unshaved, and looking ill, he went across the mews and bought a *News* from a paper-man who was so old that he seemed to grow into the pavement. Walking back, George read the story of the murder; the account was much the same as the one in the *Evening Cry*. There was one paragraph absolutely identical with that in Rollison's paper:

> A Lagonda car, with four men in it, was seen in the nearby village of Brayling, a little time after the discovery of the crime, and the police are anxious to interview the driver of the car, and his passengers.

In the sitting-room, George read it again and again, groaned, leaned back and closed his eyes, pressing the heels of his thumbs against his throbbing forehead. The picture was even more vivid now than it had been before. He could imagine Baxter smashing the hammer down on the girl's head. He wasn't sure that it had been Baxter's arm, but it was the kind of brutality one would expect from the man.

He needed a drink. There were no spirits in the place. If only he could get a drink, just a quick one, he'd feel much better. He'd have to chance going to a pub.

He turned towards the door, which opened into a tiny, square lobby—and heard heavy footsteps coming up the stairs. He caught his breath. The footsteps stopped outside his door. He clenched his hands, waiting for the knock. His forehead was beaded with sweat and he couldn't breathe easily.

There was a sharp knock.

It jarred his whole body.

He couldn't move . . .

There was another sound, a scraping at the door, and then a clang. The letter-box—someone had pushed something through the letter-box, it was only the postman!

He hurried forward, and saw a letter on the mat. The postman was clumping down the stairs again. Shivering with cold from the reaction, George picked up the letter. On it was printed: *Odds-On Pools*. Just the usual weekly pools-form, and it had terrified him!

He gave a harsh little laugh. He would be better now. He was a fool to think that the police would suspect that he had been near the scene of the murder. Why should they? He couldn't have been recognized at the wheel; Baxter and the others certainly wouldn't give him away—they daren't. And—*he* hadn't had anything to do with the murder. Why—why, he didn't even know which house they'd visited! Baxter had been careful not to let him know that. He might be all wrong. He had jumped to the conclusion that Baxter was guilty, but the robbery he had helped in might have been at another house. He was crazy to work himself up into such a panic.

He'd shave, and go out for that drink. He was getting hungry, too. That was a good sign. And he'd forgotten that by driving Baxter and his friends he had cleared himself of debt. Last night, while waiting, he had tormented himself with the thought that he couldn't be sure that it would end with this, that Baxter might force him to do other things—blackmail him into it. Ass! Two could play that game. If there were any threats like that, he would threaten to tell the police exactly what had happened. Baxter and Harry Webb, for whom he worked, were cowards at heart. Of course they were, and they would be scared of him now. He had nothing to worry about.

In that mood, at last he went downstairs and opened the door which faced the mews.

A man drew back, his hand in the air, as if he had been stretching out for the bell.

CHAPTER VI

VIOLENCE

A SPASM of physical pain streaked across George's chest. He had a moment of sheer, unalloyed terror. The new confidence vanished as if it had never existed; he stared at the man with his lips parted, his eyes reflecting his wild alarm, his heart pounding.

"Good morning," said the man.

"Good-good-good morning."

Fool! This was a policeman, he shouldn't behave like this with the police, but—it was all up. All up. They'd got on to him within a few hours—he was finished.

"Mr. George Armitage lives here, doesn't he?" asked the caller. He was smiling—deceitful swine, grinning all over his face, just because of the pleasure he was going to get out of arresting a man. George—George could say, "Yes, you'll find him upstairs," and go away. He needn't come back. The police often failed to find a wanted man.

"Are *you* Mr. Armitage by any chance?" asked the caller.

"I—yes. Yes." George gasped out the words. His chance was gone now; this was it.

The man beamed and thrust out his right hand.

"Delighted to meet you, Mr. Armitage. And a thousand congratulations!" He took George's hand, gripped it firmly and pumped his arm up and down.

"Congratulations?" gasped George.

The caller looked a little puzzled.

"Why, yes—didn't you have our letter? I'm from *Odds-On Pools*," said the caller calmly. "My name is Smith." He produced a card. "It's my pleasant duty to take our cheques round to winners in the London area, Mr. Armitage."

The truth was beginning to dawn on George; very dimly. He shook a little with a stirring of excitement. The man —what was his name, Smith?—was smiling at him broadly. He had a round, rubicund face, and looked exactly as George had always pictured a plain-clothes policeman would look. He gave a little giggle. Plain-clothes policeman! It was crazy! *Odds-On Pools*, a cheque. . . .

"Of course, it's rather knocked you back, especially as you didn't know that I was coming," said Smith, and patted his breast-pocket. "But I've got it here, Mr. Armitage. Shall we go into your flat?"

"Er—yes, yes. Of course. Yes. Oh yes!" A dazzling vision of huge piles of glittering gold flashed into George's mind. Again he felt physical pain, but this was caused by delight, not terror. He grabbed Smith's arm and drew him inside the hall, hurried up to the landing, and took out his key. He couldn't find the keyhole because his hand was so unsteady. Smith chuckled as if this were the best joke in the world. Damn the thing, it—ah! The key went in, George opened the door.

"Come in," he said. "Come in—oh, heck! I haven't a spot of whisky in the place."

"Well, we can go and have a quick one when the formalities are over, can't we?" asked Smith. "I'll just hand you over the cheque, Mr. Armitage, get you to sign a receipt, and then you can give a message to your fellow punters. They always like to hear what the big winners have to say, you know, and to know a lot about them. We try to please. You'll get a lot of publicity over this, Mr. Armitage."

"Pub——"

"Now don't let that worry you," soothed Smith, sitting down in an easy chair.

George said thinly, "How much *is* it?"

Smith did not answer immediately, but took a wallet from his pocket and opened it slowly. He no longer smiled, but put on a solemn, almost portentous, air. George wanted to scream. Everything but the immediate present was for-

gotten now, even the twinge of alarm that the talk of publicity had given him.

"How *much*?" he demanded.

"Mr. Armitage, I'm delighted to tell you that you are
about to receive a cheque from me for the sum of thirty-six
thousand, four hundred and twenty-one pounds, seventeen-
shillings and elevenpence, all for a penny stake! And *here*
is the cheque."

He slipped it from his wallet and flourished it in front of
George's nose.

.   .   .   .   .

It couldn't be true, and yet it had happened.

Here in his hand was a pink slip of paper, and there were
the words and the figures. £36,421 17s. 11d. A fortune.
Fantastic fortune! He couldn't believe it; but there was the
cheque, there was the rubicund, smiling face of Mr. Smith,
and there on the mantelpice, unopened, was the letter which
would have told him of this fantasy. Nearly £40,000—he
was a rich man. *Rich!* Why, this money had belonged to
him *last night*. He could have repaid that stolen £1,000—
no, that *borrowed* money—and told Baxter to go to hell.

He remembered Baxter, the arm, the shadow, the
hammer.

He dropped into a chair.

"Now, don't worry about feeling a bit swimmy," advised
Smith genially. "I remembered one lady who swooned
right off, and, when she came round, she kept telling me to
go away and not tell her a tissue of lies. You'd be surprised
how different people take a fortune like this, Mr. Armitage,
but the thing is to be sensible *after*wards. Most people are,
but I have known—still, we needn't go into that, need we?
Ha, ha! I can see you're a sensible man. Once again, Mr.
Armitage, I congratulate you most heartily on your wonderful good fortune. Here's the receipt, if you'll kindly sign
it, and that's all the formalities. Easy way of winning a fortune, isn't it?"

George signed.

.   .   .   .   .

He did not take Smith to *The Three Bells*. Instead, he gave him a glass of beer and a cigarette. Smith warned him that he could expect the newspapers to send representatives to see him soon, he was sure to be mentioned in several of the papers with a dividend like that. Certainly the reporters would call that day. They hadn't yet been informed, it was the practice of *Odds-On Pools* to convey the good fortune to the winners by their own personal representatives; but the London office would be informing the newspapers about now. If Mr. Armitage *really* wanted to avoid publicity, he might like to sneak off for a day or two; winners often did that if they could. Some people couldn't bear publicity.

"Do they really slide off?" asked George eagerly.

"Oh yes, plenty of them. The papers soon lose interest. Mind you, *I'd* want to get all I could if I were in your shoes, and of course *Odds-On* will expect a statement, Mr. Armitage. Something like this . . ."

He elaborated.

George gave him a statement.

It was nearly one o'clock when Smith left, with a cheery good-bye and an admonition not to run through it all in next to no time! George watched him first from the front door and then from the window. After the man had disappeared, he turned round and looked at the cheque, which was still in his hand. It was rather crumpled, and there was a dirty thumb-mark in the top left-hand corner. £36,421 17s. 11d. He could read the figures to himself without shouting now, without marvelling. He felt a sickening sense of futility. The beautiful illusion faded. He was wanted by the police—or soon would be—and he might be hanged. And this had been waiting for him, or practically waiting. If the letter had come a day earlier he would have had no troubles.

He opened the letter.

It was just a flowery note of congratulation, and told him that Mr. Smith would be calling.

He gave a rather shaky little laugh, put the cheque in his pocket, and went out to lunch. He went to a chop-house not far from Pelham Mews, where he knew he could get a good meal. He toyed with the idea of going to the bank and paying in the cheque. He could draw against it, and he needn't return to the flat. It was quite usual to disappear. Smith had been emphatic about that, and yet—it would certainly look as if he were running away.

Better face it out.

The uncertainty would be terrible.

He went to the bank and paid in the cheque. A cashier glanced at him, started up, stared, and then gave a rather sickly smile.

"You've been lucky, Mr. Armitage."

"Very. Can I draw a hundred pounds right away?"

"Oh, I expect so," said the cashier. "I'll just have to have a word with the manager, as the cheque can't be cleared this afternoon, and your account isn't—that is, I won't be a moment, Mr. Armitage!"

Five minutes later, George left with a hundred pound-notes bulging out his wallet. The eyes of every cashier and a large number of clerks were staring at him through the grills and over the tops of the partitions which separated the cashiers' space from the clerical desks. He went out feeling curiously flat. He had plenty of money: that was the main thing, although it hadn't as yet, at all events, really exhilarated him. The other business was hanging over him like a shadow. He hadn't thought much about it on the way to the bank, but on his way back he wondered if he were being followed. He kept glancing over his shoulder. Two or three people were behind him all the time he was in Oxford Street, but they appeared to be taking no special interest in him.

They didn't follow him towards the mews.

He half expected to find reporters waiting on the door-step, but the mews were deserted. He saw the woman of the flat above him look out of the window, but he didn't acknowledge her. No matter which way he turned, she always seemed to be there today.

What a shock she would have if *she* knew!

He laughed suddenly. He was *rich*!

Cheerfulness began to flow over him again.

He ran up the stairs. There were no reporters on the landing, so he would be in to greet them when they came. Quite suddenly, hardly realizing that it had happened, he wanted to talk to someone about his fortune. Anyone—but preferably Philip. What a shock Philip would get! He'd find a way of revenging himself on Philip! He'd show the bounder, who was always flaunting his money, always so supercilious and superior, always with a new *inamorata*—that was the word Philip actually liked using!

George went bustling into the flat, banged the door, and burst into song, an air from a recent hit-show. Once he started singing, he couldn't keep quiet. He boomed the tune out as he went into the bathroom to wash his hands, kicked open the sitting-room door, his mouth wide open and a vast yodel coming forth——

And he saw a man standing against the wall with a gun in his hand.

It was a short, swarthy man.

The gun was small, but had a long barrel, and was clutched in a sallow hand and pointing at George's chest.

George missed a step, stumbled, and recovered.

He didn't speak. The man stared at him blankly. That pause could have lasted only for a few seconds, perhaps only a second, but it seemed interminable. And then he *saw* the man squeeze the trigger. There was a flash of yellow flame, bright because of the murky afternoon, and for the third time that day George felt a spasm of acute physical pain. Vaguely he realized that there hadn't been much noise, just a soft *zutt*.

Another came, with another flash.

He didn't feel any pain this time.

He didn't stumble or fall, he just stared.

The expression on the gunman's face altered; he looked down at the gun, which he lowered a little.

Out of the mists of the fear of death two things came to George. *He wasn't hurt.* The man had fired at him at point-blank range, but he wasn't hurt, that pain had been caused by the onrush of fear. The second thing was quite different —fierce, tempestuous anger. He forgot the weakness and the follies of the past few years, he was George Armitage, one of the most daring junior officers in his regiment, who didn't care a damn about danger.

He leapt forward.

The swarthy man fired again, and this time the flash was very close to George, he didn't see how the bullet could miss. But he felt nothing. He crashed his right fist into the man's face, and heard the sharp crack of knuckles on jaw. He swept his left round, driving it into his assailant's stomach. The *ooch!* as the wind was driven out sounded very loud. George snatched the gun from the other's limp fingers. He felt a livid rage, felt murderous. He gripped the gun by the barrel, and, as his assailant staggered back, smashed at his head with the butt.

"Oi!" another man said.

A hand caught George's wrist before the blow fell, and he lost his grip on the gun. The swarthy assailant dropped to the floor doubled up, and clutched his stomach. A young man with a snub nose and merry eyes looked at George reproachfully.

"You might have broken his cranium," he protested. "That wouldn't do; boys with busted pates can't talk, you know—and I think he can tell us a lot, if we go the right way about it. Hallo, George!"

George drew back. "Wha—what are you——"

"As a matter of fact, I think I'm your mascot," said Snub. "Last night I saved you from suicide, this afternoon I've saved you from murder, and possible hanging; the only thing left is accidental death, isn't it? I don't want to boast," added Snub modestly, "but I am telling you the solemn truth. Actually you really owe your thanks to those dud bullets, or whoever put blanks in the gun." He examined the gun, shaking out four cartridges. "Yes, blanks," he said. "Mystery." He turned his attention to the swarthy man, whose eyes were half-open, but who looked as if he were unconscious. "He'll be all right for a few minutes," Snub added. "You needn't look so pale about the gills, there aren't any more of his kind about."

George sat down heavily on the arm of a chair.

"You might say thanks," reproached Snub.

"I—don't understand it."

"Oh well, if I have to explain my good deed in words of three letters, here goes," said Snub. "I've been keeping an eye on you, and this merchant broke into the flat soon after you left for lunch. I didn't think he'd come for a petting party, because I know him. Had a drink in a pub with him before he came here, as a matter of fact. He had a key, and I hadn't, so it took me longer to get in. Good job those bullets were blank, or you'd now be conversing with the angels."

"But why should he——"

"That's what we want him to talk about," said Snub. "You're having a lot of visitors today, aren't you?"

There was a knock on the front door.

Snub swung round, all facetiousness forgotten.

"Oh, damn! Any idea who that is?"

"No," said George. "None at all." He couldn't think clearly now, this was a fantastic day.

"Let 'em knock," said Snub. He looked wary and worried all the same. "Not expecting the police, are you?"

"Why the devil should I be?" demanded George.

"I only wondered—ooch!" Snub flinched as the knock was repeated. "If they go on much longer, they'll have the

door down, won't they? Shall I go and see 'em? Just keep
an eye on Swarthy Sam, and if he looks like being obstre-
perous, bust him over the boko. Okay?"

"I'll—I'll watch him," said George.

Snub nodded, glanced at the semi-conscious man, and
stepped into the tiny hall.

.   .   .   .   .

Snub wouldn't have been surprised to see the police. He
was surprised to see three men, two young and one old,
crowded on the small landing. He knew that these were
not policemen or detectives, for the elderly man was very
short, and one of the youngsters was certainly below
regulation height, too.

And one of them had a camera, with a flashlight bowl
stuck on the end of a rod.

The lamp flashed, vivid light dazzled him—he hardly saw
the man touch the camera. When the light had faded, the
three men laughed heartily. The eldest stepped across the
threshold and gripped his hand.

"Congratulations from the *Evening Sun*, Mr. Armitage!"

"How are you going to celebrate?"

"Mind if we come in and get a few pictures?" asked the
camera-man.

They crowded in, pushing the dazed and bewildered
Snub backwards. The tiny lobby was too small to hold
them all, and Snub felt the sitting-room door give under
his pressure. He stood firmly, grabbed the door, and pulled
it to. He managed a weak grin.

"What's all this about?"

"Now, you needn't be modest," said the elderly man
waggishly. "We all like it when a man get a lift like you've
had. About twenty-eight, aren't you?"

"Married?" asked a youngster.

"Yes—no," said Snub. He squared his shoulders. "I may
sound daft, but what has got into you? You sound as if I'd
come into a fortune."

"Pretty good," chuckled the elderly man; "you're cool. Come into a fortune!"

"Couldn't we have a bit more room?" asked the camera-man who was at the back, half in and half out of the flat. "It wouldn't surprise me if——"

"Hal-*lo*!" exclaimed a girl.

She was young, buxom and comely. Her hair was rather untidy and her hat pushed carelessly to the back of her head; but Snub had always had an eye for a pretty face, and her arrival rather shook him. There was George and the injured assailant listening to all this, doubtless wondering what it was all about. The very last thing that Rollison would want was publicity about the attack, and if these newshounds smelt mystery or violence it would be splashed all over London before the night was out.

"What, *you*?" grunted the camera-man, who appeared to lack Snub's susceptibility.

"Just came along to have a word with the lucky man," said the girl cheerfully. She had bold, bright eyes and full lips, with the lipstick smeared a little in one corner. "Don't say he won't let us in," she exclaimed.

"Oh, he will," said the elderly man.

"My hat, what a mob of hacks!" called another man from the stairs, and he appeared suddenly, a very tall, gangling fellow with a droll expression. "Isn't he in?"

"*This* is he," said the elderly man, pointing at Snub.

, "Now look——" began Snub.

"*That's* not Armitage," said the tall man, grinning at Snub. "He's a bird called Higginbottom who works for Rollison. Rollison," the man repeated softly, and his smile disappeared. "Sure, that's who he works for."

A curious tension fell upon the crowd of reporters. It was reflected in the way they looked at Snub and then at one another, almost furtively. Snub not only sensed it, but knew the reason why. Only the girl was unaffected by the sudden change in the atmosphere, and she asked gaily: "Who's Rollison?"

"Listen, sister, you go home," said the somewhat cynical young man. "If you don't know Rollison, you've no business to be on your blatt. *Roll*ison. Some say good old Toff, some say——"

"For the love of Mike," cried Snub, "will you tell me——"

"And he *isn't* Armitage?" insisted the girl.

"No, sister," said the cynical young man. "He isn't Armitage. So you work for the Toff, do you?" he added, and sounded dreamy.

The camera-man flashed his bulb; the dazzling light blinded Snub again. The camera clicked.

"You know, this looks interesting," said the elderly man. "What's the Toff worrying Armitage for? Come on, Higgy, let's have it."

"My dear chap," said Snub, trying desperately to think of an answer which would satisfy the newspapermen, and yet not hint at the truth. He was quite sure that Rollison would dislike publicity; not for its own sake, but for the harm which it might do to the people he was helping, and the work he was doing. Even a glimmering of the truth would mean that the police would descend upon George, and there was no evidence that they were as yet interested in him. Rollison had the best of reasons for wanting the situation to remain as it was.

The tall man said: "Let's push."

"Now look here——" began Snub.

The girl reporter, with her seductive smile and bold eyes, had edged her way to the front. Now she darted forward and flung open the door. Every reporter present expected to find some secret in the sitting-room, for there seemed no other possible explanation of Snub's attitude. They stared into the room.

"Well!" exclaimed the girl.

"You know, this is going a bit too far," protested Snub mildly.

He was mild because the glimmering of an idea which

might serve his purpose shone into his mind. The one thing which would prevent him from bluffing these people was the little, swarthy man. There was a chance that George's assailant could be pressed into service, for he would not want the Press to be told that he had come to murder George. Yes, bluff was possible.

So Snub pushed into the room, and began to speak.

"Now give us two minutes, and I'll give you the whole story, folk. Armitage is only——"

He broke off.

"Armitage is only——" he repeated weakly.

"Drunk," said the cynic, and leered.

In fact, George was stretched out on the couch, with his feet hanging over one end, his right arm drooping down and almost touching the floor. By his side were two empty beer-bottles and an empty half-bottle of whisky.

There was no sign of the swarthy man.

CHAPTER VII

SNUB GETS A NUMBER

"Well, I don't know that I blame him," said the elderly man. "I'd go on the razzle if I'd just been told I'd won forty thousand quid."

"Thirty-six thousand-odd," corrected the cynic.

"That's right, be awkward," said the elderly man. "My hat, he looks in a mess, doesn't he?"

"Must have known about it last night," said one of the others. "He's had a proper binge."

The tall man who had recognized Snub now turned his attention to him. Snub was standing and grinning somewhat inanely at George. George was breathing stertorously and looked as if he were flat out after a binge. Snub glanced swiftly round the room. There was no cupboard in which the swarthy man could hide, no piece of furniture that could conceal him—but one of the windows was open and a curtain fluttered a little in the breeze.

"Higgy," said the reporter.

"Well, what about it?" asked Snub.

"We want a story."

"About George?" Snub rolled his eyes. "That's easy enough. Bit of a gambler, my pal George; he was never happy unless backing winners and losers and filling in football-pool coupons and what not. He deserved a piece of luck like this. Known him for years—buddies at school," lied Snub without blinking. "He's a good chap. Single. No lady friend, as far as I know, and I think I would know. There isn't much in this story for you. Oh—he had a pretty good service record. Shot up in Cyprus. Inherited ten thousand pounds or so a couple of years ago, so he's not new to good fortune. That's about all you want, isn't it?" he asked, and grinned. "Of course, you could take a picture, but I don't think that would be fair on George."

"Well, perhaps not," admitted the photographer.

"I'll get him to pose for you when he comes round, if you like," offered Snub. "I'm sorry I tried to keep you out of the room, but I really didn't want him to be seen like this, if it could be helped. I mean, a friend's a friend."

They talked for a few minutes, and then the cynic declared that he had to go and get some news, this story wasn't any use to him. The others followed, the girl and the tall man bringing up the rear.

"If there is anything else, you'll let *me* know, won't you?" asked the girl, ogling.

Snub laughed.

"Luscious, I'd do anything to get your number. What is it? And don't fob me off with a Fleet Street number, either."

The girl laughed.

"Try Abbey 03241," she said, *sotto voce.*

"Now what's this?" demanded the tall man.

"Day or night," said the girl. "Come on, Bill, I think we'd better leave him, he'll want to bathe Armitage's head. Don't forget, will you?" she asked Snub. She pressed against him and whispered close to his ear. "Abbey 03241."

"*Night and Day!*" crooned Snub. "No, I won't forget."

"We'll let ourselves out," said the girl. "You look after your boy friend."

"Okay," said Snub. "Good-bye, beautiful."

They went out of the room and he stood staring at the door and smoothing down his hair. He looked pale and rather shaken, but suddenly grinned. He had come out of it reasonably well, and although the gunman had escaped, that was not so important. Better to have lost him than told the world that the Toff was interested in George. George, of course, had let the swarthy man go, doubtless under pressure. George could now explain.

"Okay, George," said Snub.

George didn't stir.

"They've gone," said Snub. "You needn't act drunk any longer."

George kept quite still.

"George!" exclaimed Snub in sudden alarm. He took a step forward, grabbing George's arm and shaking it vigorously. George didn't open his eyes; he wasn't foxing, he was either dead drunk or unconscious. Drugs? Well, Snub decided, possibly; taken at its worst, this was a drugged sleep. It might just be collapse after a series of shocks and too much whisky.

He let George's arm fall. He wasn't too happy about this, but the noise of George's breathing was reassuring.

He went to the telephone in the corner of the room and dialled Rollison's flat. The sooner Rollison knew, the better. Unless, of course, he was out. He was spending a great deal of time these days on mysterious errands, not confiding even in Jolly.

"Rollison here," said Rollison.

"Oh, good!" exclaimed Snub. "Look here, Boss, I've been in the devil of a fix, and I'm not right out of it yet. George has come into a fortune—*Odds-On Pools*. The Press has been round in swarms, but I fobbed 'em off."

"Good man," said Rollison, without any change of tone.

"And there's something else," said Snub. "I won't go into details, but George is unconscious. I don't think he's in danger or anything like that, but I couldn't be sure. Don't you think you'd better come round?"

"It might be an idea," agreed Rollison. "But I don't want to walk into reporters. Leave a window wide open if more turn up before I arrive, will you?"

"Oke," said Snub.

"Oke," echoed Rollison. He had not shown the slightest surprise when he had heard about George's fortune, and at that recollection Snub began to smile.

There was only one Toff. . . .

Much that Cherry had said about the Hon. Richard Rollison was true, although Cherry had exaggerated some aspects
of his activities. It was not surprising, perhaps, that Cherry
should see him much larger than life, for it was his son
whom Rollison had saved from the gallows. On one thing
the *restaurateur* had most certainly been wrong, and that was
about Rollison's complete indifference to the police. It was
true that there were times when he found it wise, because
it was helpful, to investigate some crime or another without telling the police what he was doing; and at such
times he often angered and exasperated them. At heart he
disliked it; and he was not really happy about the present
situation, because the police knew nothing of what he was
doing.

It was a self-appointed task.

But he had not accepted it for the sake of flouting the
police or bolstering up his own reputation. There was, in
fact, a long and curious story behind it about which the
police knew a little. Had he been compelled to summarize
the case and its history he would probably have said something like this:

"There is, in England, a small group of criminals working
very shrewdly and carefully, mostly throughout the East
End of London. They have no speciality. They are interested in jewel robberies, bank robberies—crimes of almost
every kind and description. They do not work themselves,
but hire others. The way they force these others, all expert
criminals—cracksmen, coiners, forgers, con-men and the
like—to work for them is by blackmail. This has been done
before, but, in my opinion, on nothing like so extensive a
scale."

Here anyone who knew Rollison and his history would
have realized that he was talking with authority, and they
would not have been surprised had he gone on:

"I've heard a great deal about this in the East End. People
do tell me, you know, things that they won't tell the police.
I wouldn't say that there's a reign of terror in the East End,

or anything like it; but I would say that the criminal fraternity, and I mean the big men, not the small fry, are agitated and worried, but can't help themselves. Now I," Rollison would probably have added somewhat earnestly, "hold no brief for these big boys of the crime world, but when a rot like this starts, it affects everybody. And sitting pretty behind this business are a number of key-men who take most of the profits and few of the risks—and I don't like 'em."

Rollison had in fact hinted at something of this kind to Snub Higginbottom and to Jolly, when he had first started his inquiries. He had come, by long, slow and devious processes, to hear of the activities of a man named Old Harry. A curious fact was that no one appeared to know the man by any other name. Few had ever seen him. He was reported to have a bodyguard—which Rollison considered significant in itself—and he used an ex-boxer named Baxter for much of his work. Old Harry was certainly one of the men right behind the scenes.

After he had been asked to keep an eye on George Armitage, Rollison had discovered that George worked for a Mr. Harry Webb, for whom Baxter worked on occasions, too. Thus, George brought him into closer contact with his quarry. Through Snub, he had been watching George for some days, and had learned much more about him. That George was heavily in debt, and that he had robbed his employer: this last he had learned on the afternoon when Snub had followed George to Garron Street.

In the whole affair, the name of Old Harry was the most freely used and the most sinister.

Rollison mused over these things as he drove from the Gresham Terrace flat to Pelham Mews. He could imagine the scene at the flat when the reporters had arrived. Snub must have been in a bad spot. He was still smiling about this when he pulled up his Sunbeam-Talbot in a street near the mews, locked the doors, and then walked the remaining few hundred yards. When he reached the entrance to the mews he saw that all the windows of the flat were closed. The raid of journalists had finished, then, and Snub was dealing with George.

Snub would have sounded far more anxious had there appeared to be anything seriously the matter with George. Snub was simply puzzled; and there were plenty of puzzling features in this affair.

Rollison saw a girl step into a doorway near the building where George had his flat, but thought nothing of it. The front door was ajar. He looked upstairs. No reporters were on the landing. He hurried up and the door opened as soon as he reached it.

Snub beckoned eagerly.

"How's it going?" asked Rollison.

"He's just about the same," said Snub, wiping his forehead. "I've had one hell of a time, guv'nor! What with this and what with that—when those confounded reporters came I thought I'd had it. Everything was going so well until then. Like the whole story?"

"I'll have a look at George first," said Rollison.

George, still breathing stertorously, lay on his back. He did not make an elegant spectacle, and he looked tired and haggard. Rollison lifted his eyelids, and studied the pupils, which were contracted, but not remarkably so. He felt George's pulse, timing it with a wrist-watch, that seemed normal enough.

"Any ideas?" asked Snub.

Rollison made a close inspection of George's head, and found what Snub had missed—a slight contusion.

"Yes," he said. "He's had a crack over the head that brought on a collapse. He's been living at high pressure, and as he had a shock last night, and again over these pools, it didn't take much to flatten him. He's not in any danger, anyhow," he said. "Now tell me——"

He broke off.

Snub had heard nothing, but he saw Rollison glance towards the door. In that glance there showed all the quali-

ties which Anne Meriton had glimpsed. In his eyes was the
devil-may-care gleam which made him so remarkable.

"What——" Snub began, in a whisper.

"What's been happening," Rollison went on in a conver-
sational tone. "There's no hurry, take your time." As he
spoke he tip-toed towards the door, and now Snub heard a
creaking sound outside. He thought immediately of the
swarthy man and the silenced gun. Neither he nor Rollison
was carrying a gun, and Snub looked round and grabbed
a heavy, glass ashtray, which would come in very handy
as a weapon. Rollison was at the door by then, his hand
stretched out to open it.

He pushed it open.

A girl was standing in the little entrance lobby. She
gasped as she backed away, and held her hand to her face.
Snub went forward, knowing there was no immediate
danger.

"*Good* afternoon," said Rollison cheerfully. "Can I help
you?"

"I'd like to wring your neck!" retorted the girl in a
muffled voice, and Snub gaped at the seductive reporter
from the *Sunday Letter*.

She took her hand away from her face and touched her
nose tenderly. Already there was a spark in her eye, and
there was nothing warm about the glance she sent Snub.

"And what have I done to deserve it?" demanded Rollison mildly.

The girl said, "You'll find out." She sniffed and dabbed
again, and looked disappointed when she saw no sign of
blood. "And before I leave here I'm going to know what it's
all about," she went on. "Friend of Armitage's my grand-
mother's pet parrot." She glared at Snub. "It's something
much deeper than that, the Toff's very interested in Armitage. So is the *Sunday Letter*. Going to talk, or shall I just
guess?"

To Snub, it was the worst moment of the afternoon. He
had been so sure that he had satisfied the Press; and it

seemed he had; all but this accursed, inquisitive wench who had completely fooled him. It wouldn't greatly have surprised him had the tall man or the cynic returned, but the girl . . .

"So you're from the newspapers," said Rollison, and to Snub's astonishment he infused what sounded like enthusiasm into his voice. "My dear girl, come in—this is just what I've been wanting!"

Even the girl gaped.

"Come and sit down," urged Rollison, and ushered her into the sitting-room.

"How did you get in?"

"Someone left a key in the lock," said the girl. "The drunk, probably." She looked suspiciously at Rollison, then at George. "I took it out."

"Nice work! Don't worry about George, he's still sleeping off a carousal," Rollison said. He pushed a chair forward and produced cigarettes. "Now, you'll play ball on this, won't you? It's a scoop for you; I don't want every newspaper running the story, it might do a lot of damage. Scoop it, or no story," he added, and beamed at her. "Going to play?"

CHAPTER VIII

THE TOFF TELLS A STORY

THE girl opened her large handbag, the strap of which was looped round her shoulder, produced a note-book and pencil, and crossed her ankles. She had very shapely if rather plump legs.

"Sure," she said. "I'll play."

"Er——" began Snub, almost desperately.

"But *not* with you," said the girl. "I'll deal with the boss. You *are* Richard Rollison, aren't you?" she asked.

"Yes," said Rollison, and glanced at Snub, giving him an almost imperceptible wink, which did much to ease that young man's feelings. "You'll hardly need your note-book, Clara——"

"Say!" exclaimed the girl reporter. "How did you know my name?"

"My dear girl! I wouldn't think much of myself if I didn't know the names of the best reporters on Fleet Street," said Rollison, and reduced the girl to a state of astonished gratification. Her boisterous sophistication faded; she looked young and eager.

"Well," she said, "shoot."

"It's like this," said Rollison, leaning forward and fixing her with an intense gaze. "Every week two or three lucky people win fortunes on the pools, and wherever there is money there are parasites. Most of the prizewinners aren't used to having a lot of money, and lose their heads. Look at George," he added, and made a careless gesture towards that young man. "When he comes round he'll be ready for milking. And dozens of these parasites will be after him."

"And you're out to stop it," declared Clara.

"I wouldn't put it as boldly as that," said Rollison

61

modestly. "But there are one or two rogues who specialize in this racket. I've good reason to believe that two or three big prizewinners have been threatened with violence if they don't pay over a share of their winnings to the easy-money boys. So Snub and I are trying to find someone, like George, who'll play with us and try to lead the crooks up the garden. A kind of Pools Winners Protection Society, if you see what I mean."

"Pools Winners Protection Society—I must jot that down," said Clara, and did so. "And that's why you've come to see George Armitage. *Will* he play?"

"Probably. I'll let you know. Obviously he won't be in the mood to say yea or nay when he first comes round," went on Rollison. "But it will give you a story that the *Sunday Letter* ought to jump at. Social scandal, and all that kind of thing—fools and their money are soon parted—but I needn't try to prompt *you*," went on Rollison, leaning forward and patting her knee. "You can see all the angles of this business, they're never ending."

"Oh, sure, *I* can see," said Clara, her eyes glistening.

"That's the spirit!" enthused Rollison. "I knew you wouldn't lose half a chance. Now, let me try to bring George round, will you? I won't ask you to stay, because George hates publicity; he would probably accuse me of trying to get him into the headlines if you were here when he wakes up." He took Clara's hands and raised her to her feet. "Satisfied?"

"Well, *thanks*," breathed Clara.

Rollison went with her to the door, patted her shoulder, and waved to her as she went down the stairs. Then he went into the sitting-room, and found Snub sitting on the arm of a chair, holding his stomach, and uttering odd squeaks.

"Amused?" asked Rollison.

"That was—gorgeous! But won't she hate you when she learns the truth!" gasped Snub.

"My dear chap, I told her the truth," declared Rollison.

Snub spluttered and then sat up, wiping his eyes. The transformation from helpless laughter to stunned disbelief was remarkable.

"I say," he protested, "are you all right? Not been hitting the high spots or anything like that?"

"George will have dozens of visitors," prophesied Rollison. "The parasites exist. Maybe there are two or three people who specialize in mulcting big money winners—I wouldn't know. But we've a chance in a million of working on George now, without the police suspecting the real reason why we're interested in him. Haven't we?" he asked mildly.

"Good—lord!" gasped Snub. "Why, it's perfect!"

"I wouldn't put it as high as that," said Rollison, "but it will help. There's going to be one big difficulty."

"What's that?"

"Sorting out the wheat from the chaff," said Rollison.

"Oh?" said Snub blankly. "Wheat from chaff?"

"Old Harry and his myrmidons being the wheat, and the parasites the chaff," said Rollison, strolling to the window and looking out. "Because George will have dozens of callers, and we shan't easily be able to tell which are which. You know, Snub, I think you've a new job."

"*Eh?*"

"Nursemaid to George," continued Rollison. "Protecting him from the leeches who will soon be trying to cling. We'll have to fix it with him, but I think he'll play."

Snub looked at George.

George's eyes flickered; he grunted and moved his head. He groaned, and let it fall back, but he did not drop off again into the stupor which had laid him out.

Before long he was sitting up, drinking black coffee with plenty of sugar in it. He had very little to say, although it was obvious that the thing which he remembered most vividly was the attack of the swarthy little man. The light relief of the reporters' visits was over; here was George, with all his good fortune, a frightened man. He said he had

been drinking from the whisky-bottle when the swarthy
man had struck him on the head with a beer-bottle.

Then, under Rollison's skilful guidance, he told everything.

.   .   .   .   .

Rollison left Pelham Mews a little after four o'clock.
There had been no more visitors, probably because the
story was not yet in the evening papers; the pilgrimage of
easy-money getters would soon begin, however. He paused
at the entrance to the mews and studied every building,
every window. It was a drab grey *cul-de-sac*. Here and
there a door or a window was freshly painted, and at two
windows were flower-boxes, bright with daffodils and
tulips, but that was the only pleasing sight. The ground
was cobbled, as it had been many years ago, when horses
had come clattering into the mews and their grooms had
washed them down and put them into their stables. This
particular mews was unusual, in that there were no garages.
The Three Bells, which could not be seen from George's
flat, had a drab sign hanging outside it, and the door and
woodwork needed painting.

Everything was quiet.

Satisfied that no one was watching George and the flat,
Rollison went on to the Sunbeam-Talbot, and drove to his
own flat. Gresham Terrace was not exactly a delight to the
eye, but there was grace about its tall, narrow, terraced
houses, the short flights of steps which led to the front
doors and the freshly painted doors and windows. Number
55G was near the Piccadilly end of the right-hand terrace.

Rollison went lightly up the stairs to his second-floor
flat.

On the flight nearest his front door there was evidence of
recent repairs. The wooden banisters had a piece let in,
and there was a large plaster patch in the wall, and a con-
crete one in the stone steps. Not very long ago, a man who
had resented Rollison's interest in his affairs had used a
little high explosive, but had failed in his chief purpose—

which had been to eliminate Rollison. Rollison did not even notice the repairs, but smiled when Jolly opened the door.

"Hallo, Jolly! On the spot as usual? Any news?"

"None, sir."

"Well, I suppose we should be grateful for that," said Rollison. "Come into the study, I want to talk to you."

Jolly followed Rollison into the room; and on being told to sit down, sat well back in his chair, knowing that Rollison would not want him to perch uneasily on the edge, as with embarrassment. He faced the desk—and also faced the trophy wall. Just as Rollison had seen the repaired staircase without noticing it, Jolly saw the trophy wall without giving it a thought—his attention was on Rollison. Yet the wall was worth close attention.

Upon it hung trophies of many crime-hunts. He had started it years before and it had become one of the traditional features of the flat. According to Snub, it was now the most photographed wall in all England.

Near the ceiling was a top hat with two bullet holes in it; this hung on a peg. And above the hat was stuck a spray of chicken-feathers, some of them stained brown—with blood. Beneath these were small cases containing tiny quantities of drugs and poisons, guns of remarkable variety, including one tiny, circular palm gun which had been used to kill at least three men, knives, including a kris and a stiletto, which had been forged centuries ago by a Milanese craftsman who had studded the hilt with small precious stones.

There were even some items which should never have been brought into the flat, but should have been used as exhibits in court when men and women were on trial for their lives. Most certainly the *pièce de résistance* was a hangman's rope, coiled up, with the noose hanging down.

Rollison finished his main story, and Jolly murmured.

"Clearly, you took quick advantage of the situation, sir, and I imagine that what you have done will be helpful. But is there not some danger of being so obsessed by a measure of success that some smaller but more important things are forgotten?"

"Which things?" Rollison demanded.

"Well, sir," said Jolly, "you have told me all this with great gusto, if I may use the phrase, but have not thought it worth while telling me how much George Armitage has confessed, nor how it was that he was careless enough to allow the swarthy man to go."

"I stand corrected," murmured Rollison. "Emphasis where emphasis is due, eh? Perhaps you're right. George was driving the Lagonda last night; he was at the scene of the murder—outside, not inside, the house. He was black-mailed into driving—and he's told us about the earlier follies which led up to it. As for the man who escaped—he had scared George, who wanted a drink, and he let the fellow outwit him."

"Well, sir," reflected Jolly. "I cannot say that George Armitage appears to *deserve* your help. He appears to be a young wastrel without any moral sense, courage or will-power."

"Probably," conceded Rollison. "And yet I rather like him. I see the man he could be, instead of the man he is. You know his service record. I suppose what you're really trying to say is that we shouldn't trust him too much."

"Precisely, sir," said Jolly.

"And I'll take your advice," Rollison assured him. He lit a cigarette and leaned back in his chair, fiddling with the cord of his monocle, which itself was slipped into his waist-coat pocket. "Now for a little summing-up. George worked for Harry Webb. Baxter, who is *Old* Harry's thug, also works for Webb. Whether Webb is Old Harry or whether the christian name is a coincidence, we don't yet know. But we do know that Baxter is our contact man be-tween the flood of crime and the syndicate profiting from it. Right, Jolly?"

"Quite right, sir, if our information is correct."

"It is. We had only heard vaguely of Old Harry before, but, thanks to George, we now know that he may be Harry Webb. Certainly, Webb has an office in the City. He is a commission agent. Very convenient kind of business, since it can cover a multitude of things legal and illegal. We also know that Baxter actually took part in last night's crime. That George was used at Harry Webb's behest. I think we'll stick to Webb and Old Harry, and assume for the time being that they're two distinct persons. However, we'd reached last night's crime."

"Yes, sir," said Jolly.

"Murder wasn't intended last night, only theft. Baxter and the men who killed the maid immediately saw their danger from George, so one man came to kill him. Through George, it looks as if we shall make a lot of progress. I can, for instance, visit Webb. There is also Philip Rowse, living in almost indecent luxury, and certainly not what the purists would call a strictly moral man," went on Rollison. "Finally, we have Anne Meriton, a most attractive young woman with a secret fear. Yesterday, we had little to go on but suspicions and hopes, today we have clues. *Clues!* And people on whose nerves to play and make a policeman's holiday. You *can't* complain now."

Rollison sat back, lit a cigarette, and prepared to listen to Jolly, who deliberated before he said:

"I have given due attention to everything you say, sir, and everything which has led up to our pursuing these investigations, and I agree that the situation is now much more promising, in that we have discovered a great deal, when hitherto it had been largely speculation. Now we do know that Baxter, George Armitage and two others were concerned in the murder of that poor girl last night. And consequently, sir, I have no hesitation in saying that in my view—and I have carefully considered every aspect of the situation, sir—you should . . ." Jolly paused, and leaned forward impressively. "You most certainly should inform the *police*."

CHAPTER IX

A PLACE FOR THE POLICE

"CERTAINLY not," said Rollison. "There's a time and a place for everything."

"Exactly, sir," said Jolly earnestly. "And I think this is the time and place for the police to be consulted. I can see absolutely *no* reason why you should put yourself in danger and submit yourself to the condemnation of the authorities because of Mr. Armitage. He has asked for everything that has happened to him—this isn't a *worthy cause*, sir, that is the point I wish to make."

"The rehabilitation of a young man could matter."

"The risk is too great, sir. After all, if you do not pass the information on to the police, they could rightly say that you are withholding *material* information, and that might be construed as obstructing the police in the course of their duty." Jolly eased his collar; there could have been no clearer indication of his earnestness. "Let the police know, sir. If they fail to achieve results after what you can tell them, then no blame attaches to us. I beg you to consider most earnestly what I have said," pleaded Jolly.

Rollison said, "Yes, Jolly, of course." He stood up, stubbed out his cigarette, and walked to the window, leaning against it. "And you're three-quarters right, but there are two points you haven't really thought about. In the first place, the fears of Anne Meriton. You know that I arranged for a private detective to follow her, don't you? To work on her fears, and make her more ready to talk."

"Sir, if we allow an attractive young woman to influence us in such an affair as this——" began Jolly.

"Oh, not her looks. Her fears. Can the police get any

68

information from her? I doubt it, but I think she will soon turn up and ask our advice. But she isn't the most important factor. This is: George was taken out on that job last night to act as a stooge. The police *might* find Baxter once they know he was concerned, but he'll lie very low. If they found Baxter, they might get from him to Webb, even to Old Harry. Even if they did, that's probably as far as they would get. But there exist these unknown men behind Webb and Old Harry, Jolly. The unknowns worry me most. George on his own isn't enough to keep me from telling the Yard. Anne Meriton and George together aren't quite enough. But when, in addition, there are these shadowy unknowns who, if the police move now, will probably fade away and never be caught—it makes a case for the lone hand."

Rollison stopped, but Jolly did not speak.

"Not convinced?" asked Rollison.

"No, sir, I cannot say I am," said Jolly; "but I have no doubt you will consider what I have said. When *will* you consult the police, sir?"

"When I'm certain that they can do a better job," said Rollison. "I won't wait a moment after that. Jolly, I want some visiting-cards," he went on; "the kind reserved for bad men."

"Very well, sir," said Jolly resignedly.

For the next five minutes they were busy, one at each side of the desk. They drew swiftly on the backs of some of Rollison's visiting-cards. The pictures were very simple and neat; they did them swiftly, showing evidence of long practice. On the back of each card there appeared a man's face—or, rather, the impression of a face. A top hat, a monocle, a cigarette jutting from a holder; a picture, it could be said, of a toff: or the Toff.

There had been a time when Jolly had regarded the use of these cards as an almost boyish prank. He had come to respect them, for he knew that they helped the Toff to create in the minds of bad men that uncertainty, alarm and even fear which made them jumpy and nervous, and ready victims.

Jolly knew another thing.

Rollison had not yet told him the whole reason for his refusal to tell the police about George. And he was preparing an onslaught on Old Harry, through Webb's office.

.   .   .   .   .   .

The offices of Harry Webb, Commission Agent, were in an old building in the City, and the building was in one of the countless dingy squares, approached by a narrow lane— there was only room for one car to move along at a time. Rollison reached the building just after five o'clock. Early dusk had descended upon London; it was more like a day in November than in April. Lights glowed at many windows of Raffety House, although it was not yet late.

Rollison parked the car near the front entrance, which was narrow and gloomy. There was no light on in the hall and, of course, no lift. A musty smell met him as he stepped over the threshold, and a floorboard creaked. There was a large notice-board by the side of one of the doors, and Rollison screwed up his eyes and read down the names until he saw:

Fourth Floor: Harry Webb & Co.

He walked up the first flight of stairs. A typewriter was clattering away near by, and he heard people talking. A telephone bell shrilled out, and a man shouted "Hallo!," but all this was happening behind closed doors. Nevertheless, it told Rollison that sounds could easily be heard in Raffety House. He reached the first landing, which was murky and seemed filled with mist. That was partly because there was a dim light on the next landing. He reached this; three more flights, and he would be at the top.

He mounted to the third landing.

The light below went out.

He stood in darkness only slightly relieved by the faint glow of fading daylight which came from the hall and windows. He looked downstairs, but could see and hear nothing now, everything was quiet up here. The light might have failed, or might have been switched off by accident, or a fanatic on saving electricity might have been on the war-path: but he could not rid himself of a feeling that this might be connected with his visit.

He went on.

The stairs creaked eerily, the sounds magnified in the quiet. He could see no light at all above him, and surely there should be light in the offices of Harry Webb, light which should shine at the sides of the door?

He paused on the top landing.

It was strange, but a fact, that this journey, from the time he had reached the front hall, had been laden with suspense and uncertainty. It wasn't at all what he had pictured: a brisk visit to sum up Webb's personality. He was not exactly alarmed, but was very wary.

He could just see the outlines of the doors on either side.

He took a pencil-torch from his inside coat-pocket and switched it on. The narrow beam of light seemed very bright. He read the name of the firm on one door, and then on the other—and the second door was marked, '*Inquiries*'. But there was not a glimmer of light when he switched the torch off.

He tried the handle of the 'Inquiries' door; it was locked. So was the other. He stood for a moment, smiling faintly, no longer on edge. Webb seemed to have fled, probably because he was afraid of what would happen if George broke down and told the police of the previous night's escapade. But that did not mean that he should turn round and go back, admitting a rebuff. There might be much of interest to be found in the office of Mr. Webb, and, in any case, he could turn a secret visit to advantage.

He took a penknife from his hip pocket.

One blade was officially a pipe-cleaner, but it was much more than that; any cracksman or policeman would have thought it suspiciously like a skeleton key. Rollison was smiling to himself in the darkness as he drew on his gloves, and then inserted the blade in the lock of the door marked 'Private'. Judging from what he had seen in the torchlight, the lock would be an easy one to open.

Metal clicked on metal.

The lock turned.

Rollison pushed the door gently open and stepped inside. It was very dark here, but a window overlooked a lighted room across the narrow square, and he could pick out the shapes of filing-cabinets, desk, two typewriters, and a tray on which were several cups and a milk-bottle, close to the window.

Only one door led from this office.

That was also locked.

This lock was more formidable than the first, and Rollison examined it closely in the light of the torch, turning his back to the window so that the light could not easily be seen from across the way. He tried the skeleton key, but the tool was not strong enough.

He had plenty of tools in his car.

He closed the knife and slipped it into his pocket. The silence was complete now, there was not even a rumble of traffic. He thought that the absence of Mr. Webb and his staff at this early hour was significant; while it was probable that Webb had removed anything which might incriminate him, Rollison was more than ever anxious to get into that private office.

He opened the door and stepped on to the landing.

A faint scuffle of movement gave him a split second's warning of what was coming, but not enough. He felt a terrific blow on the back of his head, and pitched forward into unconsciousness.

·   ·   ·   ·   ·

At half past eight that night Jolly saw a car draw up outside, and, without troubling to make sure that it was Rollison's, went into the hall. He was smiling much more freely than Snub or Rollison ever saw, because he was relieved; Rollison had been out much longer than Jolly had expected.

He waited until he heard footsteps on the top stairs.

Then he opened the door.

A man he did not know stood there.

"Good evening," said Jolly.

The man didn't speak, but thrust a letter into his hand and turned away. Jolly frowned, and drew back into the hall. He was more concerned with his disappointment than with the letter—until he saw, to his surprise, that it was addressed to himself.

He slit it open neatly, and looked inside.

Half a dozen of Rollison's visiting-cards, those reserved for bad men, were inside. Those they had prepared that day.

.   .   .   .   .

Rollison was coming round.

He did not remember what had happened, he was conscious only of the pain at the back of his head and across his eyes. When he moved, the pain grew worse. He knew that he was sitting upright, and in complete darkness, but he hardly wondered why, because the aching in his head was so severe.

He began to recall what had happened.

The scuffle and the blow, coming out of the darkness and with only the momentary warning, had come at a time when he had not dreamed there was danger. He had greatly underestimated Harry Webb. But there were things which relieved his plight. Jolly, for instance, knew where he had come, and would get alarmed if he were away too long.

Jolly . . .

No use relying on Jolly, or Snub, or anyone else. He had walked into this, and would have to get himself out. He might be anywhere—in a box-room, in an attic, in a cellar. Somewhere large, somewhere small.

At least he could find that out.

He stood up slowly, discovering in the process that he had been sitting in an armchair. A spring clanged as he reached his feet, and startled him. He grinned wryly to himself, and took a step forward.

He touched nothing.

Two—three—four—five—six steps.

This was odd. Whatever room he was in, he might have expected by now to kick against something, or at least brush against it. This room seemed to be quite empty. There was no smell of fustiness, as there might have been in a cellar. Everything was fresh and airy, and it was quite warm. He took his seventh step, arms thrust forward like a man playing blind-man's-buff. He might go on like this for a long time, and wished he had the confidence to move more quickly.

The eighth step——

He trod on the air, lost his balance and fell.

For an alarming second he thought he was falling from a great height; in fact he didn't fall far. He jolted himself badly as he spread-eagled on the floor, and he banged his head. The pain was sickening.

He got up slowly and painfully.

He turned and stetched out his hands, and touched the top of a platform—the higher level from which he had fallen. It was waist-high, so he hadn't fallen very far or done himself much harm. But it had shaken him badly, and he leaned against the ridge, gripping the edge, half wishing that he hadn't left the sanctuary of the chair.

He felt something warm.

He couldn't understand what it was at first—it was as if the air had suddenly become warmer. Nonsense! He was near a fire or a radiator. It wasn't the fierce heat of a coal fire; there was no hiss and roar of flames either, he needn't fear that the room he was in was ablaze, and yet the warmth filled him with uneasiness. His head steadied a little.

He began to move again.

He felt a soft caress on his cheek—not from a hand, just a

breath of wind. Cool, refreshing—as if he were standing by an open window. Yes, that was it—he might have been standing at an open window, looking over a sunlit lawn, with the sun and the spring wind caressing him. The illusion was so strong that he could almost picture the lawn and the trees beyond.

He laughed again, more convincingly this time, and turned with his hand still outstretched. The warmth undoubtedly came from an electric fire, and the wind probably from a fan. There wasn't much point in having both fire and fan switched on at the same time, but there it was. Fire . . .

Nonsense!

If there were a fire he would be able to see it.

He felt a swift spasm of alarm, and stood quite still, his heart thumping. It was a long time before he was steady enough to move again, or to think clearly. Of course there was no fire, there must be a radiator; naturally he couldn't see it in this darkness.

Then he heard footsteps.

They weren't far away. A man and a woman were talking too, in low-pitched voices. He moved more quickly than before, and barked his knuckles on something which hurt. He winced and shook his hand, then groped for the 'something'. He felt the iron edge of a window, as well as the cool glass. So he was standing at a window.

The man and woman were drawing nearer. Now he could hear what they said.

"Isn't it glorious?" said a girl.

"The first real day of spring," said a man.

Rollison did not give a thought to the voices, only to the words. He was clutched in the grip of a terror which seemed to paralyse him, for—he *was* at a window. The warmth came from the sun, the caress from the wind—the window was open or he wouldn't have heard those voices so clearly. It was a fine spring day . . .

And he couldn't *see*!

CHAPTER X

BLINDNESS

ROLLISON did not move.

The couple passed and their footsteps faded. They had said nothing after those few casual words—and he hated the memory of each word. He tried to find another rational explanation of what had happened, but knew there wasn't one. He was blind.

He mustn't panic.

What would happen if he shouted out, to attract the attention of the couple? Who were they? Where——

He didn't ask himself the second question, for a flash of recollection came; he had heard the girl's voice before. It was Anne Meriton, in the grounds of the house where he was a prisoner.

But he might not be a prisoner, as such.

He might have been found, injured, blinded, and been sent to a nursing-home. That was at least possible. And yet—if he were like that, surely they would have put him to bed? His head hurt, as if he had not long recovered consciousness after a blow; that could surely only have happened recently. Well, yesterday.

He put his hand to the back of his head.

He might still be suffering from the blow; even if it had happened days, even weeks, ago.

He felt a patch of adhesive plaster and some lint. His scalp was very tender when he touched it. The wound had only recently been patched up, so it hadn't happened long ago. Then he ran his hand over his chin. There was more than a day's stubble there—well, a little more. He couldn't really be sure whether it was one day's or two. In any case, that was no argument to convince him that he was free, or even that he was a prisoner; he just didn't know.

He turned away from the window, and stepped forward with his arms outstretched again. He wanted to sit down. The shock of the discovery had made the pain in his head worse, and he was weak from it. He groped for the chair, found it, placed it behind him and sat down. He was sweating from head to foot now, because of the horror of his discovery—because it was broad daylight and he couldn't see.

There could be no torture worse than this.

He groped towards his pocket and found his cigarette-case. He fumbled with the catch. Normally he would flick it open in a flash; one didn't realize how much one depended on sight, how one took it for granted. He touched the catch and the case opened. Then he had to feel inside, to make sure that cigarettes were there, he couldn't *see*. A tiny thing like this made him realize the awfulness of his plight, but he tried to shake that feeling off. He took a cigarette out, put it to his lips, then felt for his lighter.

He flicked it.

But he couldn't *see* the end of the cigarette.

He caught his breath.

Then he raised the lighter and thrust his face forward, pushing the cigarette as far away from his nose as he could. He held his hand near the lighter; touched the flame, which stung him. Keeping his finger close to the flame, so that he could feel its warmth, he touched the end of the cigarette with another.

He drew the lighter forward.

He drew in his breath.

No, he wasn't drawing in smoke. He shifted the position of the lighter a little, and then felt the smoke coming through the cigarette. He took the lighter away—and dropped it.

He felt it touch his foot, then fall dully on to the carpet.

Lighting the cigarette had done two things: it had finally

convinced him of the truth that he was blind; and it had
made him concentrate on a little task. Now he bent down
and groped for the lighter, found it and slipped it into his
pocket. He touched the cigarettes, counting aloud. "One,
two, three, four, five, six, seven, eight." Eight—that was
all. He closed the case, put it in his pocket, and smoked in
silence for some minutes, trying not to think too much. Yet
the truth kept surging over him. It might be the result of
the blow, or—*they* might have deliberately blinded him.

This wouldn't do.

He must keep quite calm.

The other problems remained: that of George, Webb,
and 'they'. This was a move in the war which he had
started. He remembered Jolly's plea that he should consult
the police, and he chuckled. That little laugh did him a
world of good, because he knew that he was seeing things
in their right perspective again.

The cigarette was nearly finished. He could feel the
warmth from the glowing tip. That created another prob-
lem—he must put it out. He could drop it and tread it into
the carpet, but that wasn't good enough for what he wanted.
It would be a minor triumph over this sudden infirmity if he
could find an ashtray.

He leaned forward, groping for the table; it was quite
near. He spread out his hand and moved it over the
polished surface. He touched a book; another, which he
pushed over the edge, so that it dropped heavily to the floor.
He didn't give up, but felt more carefully, and he touched
something cold—probably made of glass. Yes, this was an
ashtray! He held it close to his face, took the cigarette out
of his mouth and stubbed the end. Then he tried to put the
tray back, but it hit the edge of the table and fell to the
floor.

He heard another sound, and this one did not come from
outside. It was as if a door were being opened. He stared
towards the direction of the sound, and another surge of
panic came over him. He had no idea who was coming in—

couldn't even be sure that anyone was there, it might have been fancy. Or the window might have closed in the wind.

No! He heard a footstep near by. He sat absolutely still, listening; and heard the sound of breathing. A man or a woman was in this room with him; the stealthy entry was calculated to frighten him. Probably the other was grinning at him in his helplessness. But—someone was here, it was better than being alone.

Silence . . .

No, that soft breathing continued.

Was it a man? Could it be an animal? A dog, perhaps—even a cat. No, that was an absurd thought, he mustn't let foolish ideas get into his head. He relaxed a little and automatically put his hand in his pocket for another cigarette. He had the case out before he realized that lighting a cigarette would simply show the other his helplessness, and give the man reason for gloating. He put the case back. Would the man never speak? Would he be able to last out in this self-determined battle of wills?

Then a roar of sound smashed the silence, a deafening explosion near his ear, which made him start so violently that he slipped forward in his chair. His head was ringing, aching far more than ever; the explosion couldn't have been many inches away from him. He tried to get back on the chair, but it slipped from under him and he fell heavily to the floor.

That had been a shot.

"Nervous, Rollison?" a man asked.

So he'd won, he'd made the man speak first. It was a silly thought, absurd to talk about winning at such a time as this, but—there it was. He didn't try to get up, but straightened his legs and looked upwards towards the sound of the voice.

"Yes," he said. "It's a family complaint."

"I don't know about that," said the man who had fired the shot, "but it's a complaint you're going to get very badly."

"Well, I'm used to it," said Rollison.

The man did not make any further comment, but he no longer tried to move silently. A spring twanged; the spring in an armchair, *the* armchair—no, it couldn't be that one, it was on the platform. He heard a match scrape, and smelt tobacco—the rich smell of a cigar or a cheroot, not a cigarette.

"Rollison," said the man.

"Speaking," said Rollison. But he told himself that he must be careful not to be puerile. Scoring silly points in a wordy battle wasn't going to help him.

"Do you know me?" the man asked.

"I know so many people," said Rollison.

He heard a movement, but didn't expect the ringing blow on the side of his head which knocked him to one side. He banged his head on a table or a chair. He couldn't think or speak, he was so full of pain.

The other gave him some time to recover. The smell of cigar smoke grew stronger.

"Don't be clever," the man said at last. "Do you know me?"

"Not yet," said Rollison.

"I hope that's true."

"It's perfectly true," said Rollison, "but I hope to recognize you the next time we meet."

The man didn't respond to that, but said in a satisfied voice: "I didn't think you'd got very far. What put you on to Old Harry? Was it Armitage?"

"I heard rumours about Old Harry before seeing George," said Rollison. "I knew about boy-friend Baxter, too."

"Well, that won't help you any," the man said. He laughed—an ugly little sound which had menace in it, and yet Rollison did not think the laugh was directed towards him and his plight. "Who else do you know, apart from Baxter and Old Harry?"

"A little chap who came to shoot George," said Rollison.

"Who else?"

"Webb," said Rollison softly. He heard the other catch his breath; so he had scored a point, for that involuntary pause surely meant that Webb and Old Harry were two different people.

"So you know Webb isn't Old Harry," the other said at last. "It was certainly time we stopped you. Do you know anyone else who worked with or for Old Harry?"

"Not for certain."

"Do you know anyone else?" said the man, and his voice was harsher now.

Rollison said, "I know a Superintendent Grice, of New Scotland Yard, and some other policemen who are extremely interested in what——"

He broke off, for the man clutched his throat. The powerful fingers tightened their grip. He realized then how completely helpless he was, unable to anticipate a move or to prepare for one—an easy victim to such third-degree methods as this.

"Rollison, don't *lie*. You've handled this on your own— you thought you were big enough to do it. You haven't told the police."

Rollison didn't try to speak, even when the grip relaxed slightly. He could feel the other's breath on his cheeks, and the smell of cigar smoke was very strong. Yet he had learned something of importance: this man was frightened in case he had told the police.

"Have you?" the man growled.

"You'll find out in due course," said Rollison. He expected a third blow, but it didn't come. He rested his hands on the carpet and prepared to spring to his feet—it would give the other a surprise, and he would feel better if he were standing. "The one thing you can be quite sure about is that you *won't* get away with this little game," he said—and jumped up.

He thought for a moment that he would fall; there was nothing on to which he could hold to get his balance. He swayed backwards, but managed to recover and stand still.

The only reaction from the other man was a gasp of surprise—he didn't touch him again.

"Got a little food for thought?" demanded Rollison.

"You've asked for more trouble," said the other roughly. "Rollison, how much have you told the police?"

"I should ask Jolly," said Rollison.

"*Who?*"

"Jolly, my man," explained Rollison. "Or Snub, who's looking after George. Or some of my other friends—I wonder how many of them you know. People call them toughs because they come from the East End, but—they don't like you and your friends. Ever thought how silly it is to make enemies of East Enders?"

"They're a lot of illiterate fools," growled the other. "They do what they're told. Rollison . . ."

He paused, as if to collect his thoughts. He could not guess how much good he had done Rollison now—how significant were the words 'They do what they're told'. That was a virtual admission that this man was one of those who blackmailed crooks into working for them. It was the second point gained; the success invigorated Rollison.

The man said more quietly: "Rollison, I'll give you an hour to think this out, then I want the whole truth—just how much you know, how much you've told the police, how much your friends know. If you aren't ready to talk, then you'll get such a bashing you'll never be the same again."

"Nice chap, aren't you?" murmured Rollison. "However, there are ways and means of dealing——"

"And don't be so clever!" roared the man, and struck him again. Rollison staggered back, knocked against the table, but managed to prevent himself from falling. His head was hammering; he thought he heard footsteps, but wasn't sure. The door slammed.

He felt suddenly weak. The man had gone; his hour's grace had started, and in that hour he would have to decide how much to say, and how to convince the fellow that what he said was true.

Soon the real horror of his plight came back, reminding him of his helplessness. What use was there in defiance now? He knew so little. It wouldn't help to pretend that he had confided in the police; it might even help him if he could convince his tormentor that the police knew nothing. He stood quite still, his head throbbing, the circumstances crowding upon him—and as he stood there he heard a telephone bell ring.

Someone answered it—not far from the door.

He didn't hear what was said, but heard hurried footsteps, and, after a few seconds, a door open downstairs. He heard the hum of a car engine, and a man—*the* man—call out: "I'll be back to dinner."

So he would be away for several hours.

That was the first relief that Rollison had felt since the man had shown his hand. In a few hours he might be able to think of some way of striking back. Certainly he would be able to collect himself, to decide on the best course of action.

His thoughts were swift now, touching every aspect of the situation—and he was still wondering how he could bluff his tormentor when he felt a sudden draught, then heard the door close.

Someone else had come into the room.

CHAPTER XI

FRIENDLY VOICE

ROLLISON stared towards the door.

Someone walked lightly towards him, and stopped not far away. He felt his pulses beating fast, but tried to look composed. He couldn't even be sure that he was looking towards the newcomer.

Then Anne Meriton said, "So it *is* you."

Her voice was quiet, tinged with what might have been sympathy. Rollison could imagine her standing there, and the strange composure with which she cloaked her fears. But, above all things, she spoke in a friendly voice.

"Yes," he said. "The guinea-pig, I think. Would you mind helping me to a chair? An easy one, for preference."

"Hold out your hand," she said.

Her fingers were cool and firm. She led him a few steps, and then said, "Turn half-left." He obeyed. "You can sit down," she said. He did so, and heard the whang of the spring. This was the chair in which his tormentor had been sitting.

"Would you like a cigarette?" she asked.

"Please."

A lighter clicked. He felt her fingers on his cheek, and then a cigarette was put to his lips. He held it fast, and drew in the smoke—and at that moment he realized what the feeling of nausea had concealed before: he was hungry. But he was sitting at ease, smoking, and there was no need for such tension as he had felt with the man. He wondered if Anne was sitting or standing. The lighter clicked again, so she had started to smoke.

"Thanks," he said belatedly.

"You know, don't you, that you are in a terrible position?" said Anne.

"I'm not so happy as I might be," said Rollison, "but I have been in awkward spots before."

"I don't think you can ever have been in one as serious as this," said Anne. "Are you *quite* blind?"

"As blind as if I were in a dark room," said Rollison.

She caught her breath.

He began to wonder why she had come, what she was doing at this place at all. It seemed ages ago since he had talked to her at Cherry's, yet it had only been the previous day—or, at most, two days ago.

"I'll tell you what I can," said Anne quietly.

"How long have I been here?"

"Not very long."

"Where am I?"

"In a house in the country."

"Is it isolated?"

"Yes, it is rather."

"Where's the nearest village?"

"About two miles away," said Anne.

"And the main road?"

"Quite as far. The nearest other house, as far as I know, is a mile and a half away, and that's a farm-house. It's no use thinking you've any chance of getting away."

"I hadn't got as far as that," said Rollison. He was glad that she had answered frankly; at least he knew something of the background. "Why did you come to see me?" he asked next.

"He's gone out, and it seemed a good chance," she said. "I wanted to warn you—*not* to fight him."

Rollison did not speak.

He stretched out his hand, and she touched it. Her fingers were cold, an indication of her intensity. She didn't continue immediately, but he imagined that she was staring at him with those lovely, blue eyes. They were clear and

frank and yet shadowed with fear—unless he had been
mistaken.

She might have fooled him completely, and might be
fooling him now, pretending sympathy so as to gain his
trust. At least he mustn't disregard the possibility of that
old trick. 'He' might have recognized a stubborn spirit, and
decided that he was more likely to get results this way than
by threats and force.

"You can't win," she said, and he could only just hear
the words, she spoke so softly. "You haven't a chance—
look what they've done to you."

"Ah, yes," said Rollison, "but look what I've done to
them."

"Oh, don't be silly. You haven't hurt them at all, and
they've—blinded you."

"Well, we needn't weep tears over that," said Rollison.
It was surprising how easy it was to speak calmly while his
heart was thumping, and real fear of the blindness welled
up inside him. He went on as easily as he could: "It's been
done before, you know. Blindness can be induced, temporary blindness which——"

"They'll make it permanent if you don't do what they
want," said Anne. "Be advised by me, don't try to fight.
I've tried——"

She broke off.

Rollison said softly: "It's a bad thing to give up a fight,
you know. It saps the will and destroys courage and rots
one's self respect. Why don't you tell me why you're so
frightened? Why you're here—doing what 'he' tells you?
Anne, even if you and I stop fighting, others will take it up.
My friends—the police—others we don't even know. 'He'
can't win. We can lose, but we needn't, and even if we do,
should we manage to weaken his position a little, then we've
done some good and made it easier for the others. That's
true, isn't it?"

She didn't speak.

"Isn't it?" insisted Rollison.

She said, "I've fought for so long, it's no use now." There was a catch in her breath, and he felt convinced that she was sincere, this was no trick. "Please don't make the same mistake that I did. . . . So many people will suffer, and——"

She stopped abruptly, and jumped up—he heard her movement. Her hand left his. He thought that she was now standing and staring at something. He could hear her heavy breathing.

She didn't speak.

Footsteps approached. . . .

Another sound—as of a slap. Anne gasped, and Rollison knew then that someone had entered the room, approached her, and, without speaking, had slapped her across the face. Stumbling sounds followed. He could imagine the newcomer pushing her towards the door.

It slammed.

The footsteps outside faded quickly, and he was left alone again.

.   .   .   .   .

Snub Higginbottom was a very worried young man, and his anxiety was the greater because there was little he could do to relieve it. His task was to look after George. There were advantages about that, for George, now on the heights of delight and now in the depths of despair, was an interesting study. So were some of the people who came to see him —Rollison's prophecy had soon come true. But, to Snub, the welfare of George Armitage was a trifling thing compared with the welfare of Richard Rollison—and there had been no word from Rollison for twenty-four hours.

George was sitting at a small writing-bureau, reading letters. He was having one of his good spells, when everything in the world was bright.

He threw back his head and laughed.

"It's incredible," he said, turning round and beaming. "I've had—how many letters?"

"One hundred and three," said Snub, "and more will come by every post. You're famous."

"I'm rich," said George simply. The phrase was on his lips dozens of times a day. "Believe it or not, that's what matters. Oh, boy! And now listen to this one."

A sharp rat-tat on the outer door made him stop.

"Hallo, another caller," he said. "All right, I'll go."

He was nearer the door, and hurried to it. Snub stood up and followed him slowly. At the back of his mind lingered the possibility that the friends of Baxter might be driven to such desperation that they would send someone to make a bare-faced attack on George. Therefore he much preferred to open the door himself, but there was nothing he could do with George during these exuberant moments. So he stood just inside the sitting-room.

"*Good* evening!" boomed George, "and what can I do for you?"

"I would like to see Mr. Higginbottom, if you please," said the caller, in a tone doubtless calculated to take George down several pegs.

It was Jolly, and Snub went forward hopefully.

"Any news?" he asked eagerly.

"I am afraid not," said Jolly.

"News?" echoed George. "What about?"

"You wouldn't understand yet," said Snub, stepping back into the sitting-room. "Come in, Jolly. This is Mr. Armitage—Armitage, this Mr. Rollison's valet."

"Oh-ho!" exclaimed George.

They went into the sitting-room, and George stared with undisguised wonderment at Jolly's solemn face. Anxiety had created a myriad more lines and wrinkles, and Jolly walked stiffly. He was neatly dressed in black, and his funereal manner made him look like a mourner. He bowed politely to George, but could not entirely conceal his disdain.

"No, Mr. Higginbottom," he said, "there is no news of Mr. Rollison, and it is now more than twenty-four hours since he left the flat. I must admit that I am greatly perturbed."

George said, "Here, what's this?"

"The boss went to see your pal Webb, and hasn't turned up again, yet," said Snub. "What's worse, some things he had in his pocket were returned to the flat last night. Not a good sign."

"Good lord!" said George blankly.

"I really cannot see how we can delay taking action any longer," said Jolly. "I feel sure that had he wished us to remain inactive he would have sent a message of some kind. I have never been happy about this affair—never."

"Look here, why haven't I heard about this before?" protested George.

"Didn't want to worry you," explained Snub.

"That's all very well," said George, sounding indignant. "There are limits to what you ought to keep from me. Damn it, Rollison is in this largely to help me——"

"I am glad you appreciate that," said Jolly icily.

George flushed.

"Perhaps I haven't talked much about it," he said, "but I'm not a blind fool. And if it hadn't been for Snub I should have had it yesterday afternoon. Look here, are you serious? He really went to see Webb? Have *you* seen Webb?"

Jolly said quietly: "Yes, I visited the office this morning, at ten o'clock. If Mr. Rollison went straight there last night he would have reached there about a quarter to five. I am told that the office was open until 5.30, but that Mr. Rollison did not appear. Webb himself was away, so according to my informant they could not have met in any case. I have made further inquiries," went on Jolly, "and I cannot find any inconsistencies in that story. The offices, as you know, are on the top floor of Raffety House; no one in any of the other offices appears to have seen Mr. Rollison or heard anything unusual. But his car, the Sunbeam-Talbot, was seen by at least three people—a typist, an office boy and a solicitor—between half past four and five o'clock last evening. There is no doubt at all that Mr. Rollison went to the

building, although he appears not to have visited the top
suite of offices."

"Haven't you told the police?" asked Geoge.

Jolly looked at him through his lashes. There was something about that long, cold appraisal which made George
flush again. Snub shook his head and thrust his hands
moodily into his pockets.

"No," said Jolly.

"Why not?" demanded George.

"I should have thought that question, coming from you,
to be quite superfluous," said Jolly coldly.

Snub broke in: "Tell 'em about the boss, and we may
have to tell 'em about you, George," he said flatly. "The
great man didn't want us to. I don't mind admitting,
though, that we haven't reported him missing because we
know he'd want us to give him a run, and not only because
of the effect it might have on you."

"Oh!" said George. His voice was weak. "I see."

Jolly continued to look at him disdainfully, in fact contemptuously. George flushed again. Snub went moodily
towards the window and looked out.

.   .   .   .   .

For George, it had been a memorable day; unreal in
many respects. He had started off by thinking that the
police were bound to come to see him during the day, and
he had been on edge throughout the morning. Caller after
caller had arrived, including more reporters and an incredible number of smooth-tongued, suave-looking mendicants
—for whatever excuse they offered, these had all come to
beg, or to put up glowing 'propositions' which needed just a
little finance. In this dream world of mingled excitement,
exhilaration and gloom George had floated freely—and,
from the beginning, one thing had reassured him.

Rollison.

He had heard much of the Toff, and Snub had told him a
great deal more the previous evening. He had built up a

thickening smoke-screen of security because this almost
legendary figure was on his side. After all, he *hadn't* killed
that girl. Rollison knew that, and had agreed that it was
wise, for the time being, not to tell the police exactly what
had happened. The confession had taken a great load off
George's mind and conscience. He had become fully prepared, even eager, to leave the responsibility to Rollison
and, in a lesser degree, to Snub. Jolly he hadn't thought
of seriously.

He hadn't thought very deeply about anything, only
skimmed the surface.

From the moment of Jolly's arrival he had felt different,
however. Jolly's curious quality of disdain, almost con-
tempt, had got under his skin, at first irritating, then sham-
ing him. In the conversation which ensued, shame gained
the upper hand. He realized, even before the others had
put it into words, that they had not yet told the police about
Rollison partly because of him.

He looked at Jolly, who said: "I feel the matter has been
left quite long enough, Mr. Higginbottom, and no matter
what Mr. Armitage thinks, it is incumbent upon us to report the disappearance."

George growled, "You rate me rather lower than the
things that crawl, don't you?"

"Now, look here, old chap——" began Snub.

"Well, he does," said George, his face pale. "I don't
know why the devil he should. If you think I want to risk
anyone else's neck to save my own, you're damned-well
mistaken. If Rollison's in a jam because of me, I'll do everything I can to get him out—and if the best way is to have
myself locked up, all right—that's what I'll do." He strode
across the room, grabbed the telephone, and began to dial.

He reached WHI 1212, and heard the ringing sound.
Then Jolly appeared at his side and, without appearing to
use force, wrested the receiver from him.

"Allow me, sir," said Jolly.

That 'sir' altered the whole complexion of the incident.

Jolly's gift for saying much in a monosyllable was something new to George, who stared. Jolly's expression did not alter; he did not smile, but inclined his head gravely as he placed the receiver to his ear; but he had recanted much of what he had said, and made George feel much easier in his mind.

George was astounded, bewildered.

Jolly asked for Superintendent Grice, and held on. George, who should have had palpitations at the fact that the police were actually on the line, felt more genuinely easy than he had done all day. True, he had no feeling of exaltation, but there was a sense of satisfaction, of rightness. Better to get everything over, face it out, pay what he had to pay, and then start all over again.

"Good evening, Mr. Grice," said Jolly into the telephone. "Yes, it is Jolly here. I think you should know . . ."

He told Grice about Rollison's disappearance, and where he had gone, but he did not mention George. He promised to visit Scotland Yard immediately, rang off, and then turned and faced George with a faint smile.

"I see no reason why we should tell them everything at this stage, sir. If it has to come out a little later, then it should come through you. If I may say so, I think it would be wise, in that event, not to allow the police to know that we are already aware of what Baxter persuaded you to do. The—ah—story which we concocted, of protecting prize-winners from rogues and vagabonds, will serve very well, I think, for the time being. Don't you agree?"

"Well," began George. "I'm not sure——"

"Of course it will," said Snub heartily. He winked at George, and saw Jolly to the door.

George was smiling a curious little smile when Snub returned. The feeling of well-being remained; now he was at grips with the situation and with himself.

He sat down in an easy chair, poured himself out a whisky-and-soda, and then began to talk. Snub found a great deal of what he had to say almost embarrassing. George did not think much of his own recent activities. He went through the whole dismal story of the past two years, from the time he had started throwing his inheritance away and getting into debt. He could see, he said, that he had behaved like a fool, a knave, an idiot; he wasn't worth a corner of Rollison's finger-nail. He was even prepared to abase himself before his cousin Philip. Philip had been quite right.

Snub, in his wisdom, made odd remarks, grunted, smiled, or shook his head sadly, according to the need of the moment. He knew that Rollison had expected some such transformation as this, that Rollison himself would wonder whether the change would be permanent.

It was nearly dark when George finished, and poured himself out another drink. He felt drained of energy, and yet mentally rested.

"The question now is, how can I *help*?" said George.

"My dear chap, one never knows. I'm a bit glum about Rollison's long silence, but he's a remarkable customer, you know. It wouldn't surprise me too much if he turned up, or sent a message, and there'll be plenty of opportunity to help a bit later on. You just sit tight. Jolly will give the word when he thinks the moment's come for full confession——"

He broke off, for the telephone rang.

"I'll answer," said George, and stretched out for the telephone. "Yes, speaking," he said into it. "Yes—*what*?"

He gripped the receiver so tightly that his knuckles went white, and Snub jumped up, staring at him in agonized suspense.

CHAPTER XII

A CHANCE FOR GEORGE

"YES," said George again. "You have a message from Mr. Rollison, for me? Go on."

He glanced at Snub, who was now close by his side.

The woman at the other end of the line had an attractive, youthful voice; there was something familiar about it. She seemed a long way from the mouthpiece, and he had to strain his ears to catch what she said.

"Mr. Rollison wants you to meet me at Earl's Court station at seven o'clock this evening," she told him, "on the platform for the Wimbledon trains."

"How shall I recognize you?" asked George in a stifled voice.

"You know me," said the girl. "You saw me at your cousin's flat—do you remember?"

"Philip's flat?"

"Yes."

"I don't remember—oh, yes, I do! Yes, of course!" He had a mental picture of the girl, so poised and calm and yet in some odd way tense, as she had stood and watched him. She had followed him to the Embankment because she had been afraid that he had really meant to take his own life.

"Seven o'clock, then," she said. "And Mr. Rollison is most anxious that you should be alone. Please don't be late. Good-bye."

"Good-bye," echoed George.

He did not replace the receiver immediately, but stood staring at it. Gently but firmly Snub took it away, and demanded to know who it had been and what had been said. George told him quietly, still thinking of the girl. Everything about her came back with a startling vividness.

"Very nice indeed," said Snub, when the story was finished. "Trap Number One."

"Trap?" snapped George.

"My dear chap, yes. Trap to get you out of the flat and on your little own," said Snub. "Rolly might do a lot of crazy things, but he certainly wouldn't ask you to meet this girl *alone*. They'll probably try to push you in front of a train, or something quick and easy like that. Remember that I said the only other thing I can save you from is accidental death?" He gave a mirthless laugh. "You can't go, of course, but I——"

"I shall go!"

"Now take it easy," protested Snub. "We're on to something. It stands to reason, old chap, that they want to do you in. After all, you can give Baxter away, and probably do a lot more damage. They won't try again here, because they know you're on your guard. The most luscious bait is always a ripe piece of feminine lure, and seldom fails. I think she'll have a shock when I turn up instead of you. Jolly will bring up the rear, of course, and follow."

"*I'm* going to Earl's Court," said George.

"Now look here——"

"You don't know that this is a trick," said George. "It may be genuine. You saw the girl yourself, didn't you? *She* wouldn't lie."

"Oh, wouldn't she?" murmured Snub.

"I'm quite sure she wouldn't," said George irrationally. "Anyhow, it doesn't matter whether she would or not, I'm going to take a chance. It's the first time I've had to *do* something for Rollison, it—damn it, it brings to a head all that I've been saying tonight. If I turn this chance down I shall never be able to look anyone in the face again."

"Oh!" said Snub. "Like that, is it?"

He put his head on one side and eyed George very thoughtfully, trying to imagine what Rollison would decide to do in circumstances like these.

The answer wasn't difficult to find.

Rollison would let George go, and follow him closely.

.   .   .   .   .

Anne Meriton replaced the receiver and turned to the man standing by her side. He was short, swarthy, power-ful-looking, dressed well, and was smoking a cigar. They were in a Mayfair flat, and the hum of traffic from Picca-dilly came floating in at the open window.

"Did you get him?" he asked.

Anne said, "He says he'll come."

"He'd better," growled the man.

Anne said, "You promised me that if I did this you'd let—let Rollison see again."

"Well, so I did," said the squat man, and he began to laugh. "Well, so I did!"

Anne stood tense and still, very pale-faced, while he laughed more loudly.

.   .   .   .   .

The worst of the evening rush was over at Earl's Court, but there were crowds of people on most of the platforms, and two or three hundred on the platform for the Wimble-don, Richmond and Putney trains. Over the bridges there moved a constant stream of people, and the subway was continually disgorging or absorbing others.

Near a closed tobacco-kiosk George stood for some minutes, smoking, watching the nearest subway, or glanc-ing at the clock. He had been here for a quarter of an hour, and it was still only five minutes to seven.

There was no reason at all why the girl should be early.

He left the kiosk, and walked up and down the platform. The hands of the clock seemed never to move. He kept away from the edge near the line, for one thing which Snub had said had impressed him: 'they' might push him in front of a train. Astonishing how vividly that remained in his mind. But although he was cautious, he also scoffed at himself for these fears, which were the product of Snub's foolish fancy. That girl was all right; he couldn't doubt her goodwill for a moment.

Seven o'clock.

He stared at the clock, then at the subway, as he went back to the kiosk.

Two minutes past seven, and she hadn't turned up.

Perhaps something had happened to her.

Perhaps——

"Good evening," said Anne Meriton.

George's heart leapt as he swung round. She was at his side—had come from behind him, as if she had been waiting on the platform all the time. His eyes lit up, and he gripped her hand. She was obviously surprised by the warmth of his greeting.

"Hallo!" cried George. "I thought you weren't going to make it!"

"Oh, I got here," said Anne, and forced a smile. She took her hand away. "We're going on the next train to Wimbledon."

"To see Rollison?" he asked eagerly.

"Oh, we shall see him," Anne promised, "you needn't worry about that."

She looked at the indicator, then took a step forward. The next train was for Wimbledon. George went with her, but glanced right and left. She went nearer to the platform edge than he liked, and instinctively he drew back. Then he decided that he was still too deeply impressed by Snub's warning. He stepped right to the edge.

"Don't go too close," warned Anne.

George laughed; the sound was almost a giggle, and the girl looked at him in surprise. The train rumbled towards them, its lights glowing, thundered alongside the platform and slowed down. Doors opened and people streamed out. They found two seats, although there were very few free in the middle of the train.

He offered cigarettes.

"Thanks," said Anne.

"Now, what *is* this all about?" George demanded. "Where is Rollison?"

"We can't talk here," said Anne.

She was right, of course; he would have to shout to make himself heard, and the people opposite, as well as those behind and two who were strap-hanging, would overhear. He stole a quick glance at Anne, who looked straight in front of her. He saw how her long lashes curved and brushed her cheeks. She was even more beautiful than he remembered.

He glanced down at her gloved hands. He couldn't see any ring bulging beneath the finger of her glove, but that didn't mean that she wasn't engaged. After all, a creature as lovely as this was almost certainly engaged.

But—*Philip.*

She was one of Philip's *inamoratas*!

He remembered that she had denied it, and yet at the time he hadn't been sure. He had insulted her brutally when they had first met; he hadn't remembered that until now. If she wasn't one of Philip's mistresses, what had she been doing at the Garron Street flat?

At Wimbledon they got out, and through into the yard. There were several private cars waiting, as well as several taxis. George glanced at two chauffeurs who drew near, and then looked beyond them to a small two-seater, which he recognized. That was Snub's car! He saw Snub standing by the station wall, but Snub did not look at him.

Snub might upset everything. The fool!

A tall chauffeur came forward.

"Here I am, miss," he said, singling Anne out.

"Oh yes," said Anne. "Good evening, Spencer."

George handed her into an opulent Daimler. They settled down in the back, and the car moved off. George hadn't expected this. He tried to see Snub in the mirror, but couldn't get a clear view. He turned round to look through the rear window, but couldn't be sure whether Snub was just behind or not.

"How long in this?" he asked.

"About three-quarters of an hour," said Anne.

"By Jove! as long as that? Well, we'll have time to talk, anyway!"

Anne looked at him strangely.

"Mr. Rollison particularly asked me not to tell you what he wanted," she said, "and I think it's better to obey him, don't you?"

"Well—as you like," said George, acutely disappointed.

They drove on through the dusk, out of the suburbs and into the country. He could not help feeling that it was like his drive in the Lagonda. And they were going a long way. As darkness fell, he peered through the windows at the hedges, stared ahead at the glistening telegraph wires, and the tall poles which came near and then fell behind in monotonous succession. Then they turned off the main road, and there were only the hedges and the twisting, turning road in front of them.

Anne still didn't speak.

George kept looking behind him, but he couldn't see the headlights of another car. It seemed as if Snub had lost them. Well, that was probably what Rollison wanted— Snub would have been the first to agree that one could never tell what Rollison would do next.

They swung into a gateway, and the headlights shone on a square, Georgian house. The ground-floor windows were shuttered. Creeper on the walls looked very bright in the glow, so did the brass letter-box, bell and knocker. There was a pillared porch, and two steps leading to the front door.

The car pulled up, and the chauffeur jumped down and opened the door. By the time they reached the porch, the front door was open. A squat man was standing at the side, and he bowed to Anne as she entered.

George followed, and the door closed behind them.

He turned and looked at the servant.

This was the man who had held him up at the flat, who had so nearly killed him.

The man grinned.

George snapped, "This *is* a trap, then!"

"But you were very wise to come," said a stranger who appeared from one of the rooms which led from the hall; "and Miss Meriton had no choice. Armitage, she had to bring you here to see Rollison. Now you shall see him. All right, Anne," the man added, and he took a cigar-case from his pocket, offering it to George.

Anne disappeared into one of the rooms.

CHAPTER XIII

CLEAN SWEEP

THE stranger led George upstairs and into a room, a huge chamber, and an unusual one in a private house. It was more like a small theatre than an ordinary drawing-room. At one end was a stage, completely bare of furniture, although red velvet curtains draped the wall behind it. Below the stage was a thick red carpet, and this part of the room was furnished like a drawing-room, with a grand piano in one corner, luxurious easy chairs and settees, occasional tables, and in another corner a huge walnut-cased radiogram. For some reason the room reminded George of Philip Rowse's flat. It was luxurious, and just missed ostentation.

But George took little notice of the furniture and furnishings.

He looked wildly at Rollison.

Rollison sat in an easy chair, with his hands gripping the arms. There was something unnatural about him. He hadn't the poise which George had seen before, when his eyes had been so gleaming and so full of vitality. He didn't get up, and stared fixedly—at the *piano*.

George gasped, "Rollison!"

"Hallo, George," said Rollison, and he seemed to relax. "So they've brought you into the parlour, have they?" He turned his gaze towards George and the squat stranger, who had closed the door behind him and was now piercing his cigar.

"Anne said you *sent* for me," said George. He spoke quite flatly, with no feeling in his voice. "I thought she could be trusted."

"I hoped she could," said Rollison.

"She can be trusted to do the wise thing," said the squat man. "Have a cigar, Rollison."

"No, thanks."

"It will keep away the pangs of hunger," said the other.

"Hunger!" cried George.

Rollison smiled—and George was fascinated by that, by his strange, uncanny manner. He moved slowly when he moved at all, and his voice was carefully modulated, as if everything he said was an effort.

"Yes, George—they think I'll talk more freely if I've an aching void where there should be a good dinner. But they'll probably find out their mistake." He laughed. "Be warned, they're as full of tricks as a clown at a circus, only they're not so funny. Get ready for a shock."

George didn't speak.

"I can't see," said Rollison.

"You can't . . ." began George in a queer, strained voice. He didn't finish what he was going to say, but swung round on the squat man. "What the devil have you done to him?"

"Not much, yet," said the squat man smugly. "It's quite true that he can't see. It's up to him whether he ever gets his sight back—but that won't matter much if he starves himself to death," He laughed again, and George clenched his hands. "I shouldn't try to get rough," the man said, looking at him contemptuously; "you'll get badly hurt if you do, and you needn't get hurt. Come into a fortune, haven't you?"

"I——"

"It's a good thing for you," said the squat man. "I can use a promising young man with money—if he's prepared to behave himself. If he isn't—well, I dare say the police will be interested in what he did with himself the night before last. *Very* interested. Eh, Rollison?"

Rollison said, "Probably."

"You see, Rollison is a realist," said the squat man. "Now I'm going to leave you two together for half an hour, so that you can have a little chat. Don't forget what I want,

Rollison. The whole truth about how much you know and how much George knows. The *whole* truth."

He nodded to George, and went out.

.   .   .   .   .

Snub drove along the road from Wimbledon to Redhill, watching the rear light of the Daimler in which George and Anne were travelling. He hoped George wouldn't give away the fact that he had been at Wimbledon. He'd left Pelham Mews just after George, and had reached Earl's Court in time to hear the girl take a ticket for Wimbledon. Anne did not appear to have noticed him, and George hadn't shown any sign of recognition.

The Daimler turned off the main road.

Snub trod on the accelerator.

With luck, he could turn the corner and get up close to the Daimler and drive without lights. It wouldn't be easy, but it would lessen the risk of being noticed. He must find out whether Rollison was at the house where these people were going. This might have been just a trick to get hold of George; but Rollison might be there, and——

He swung round the corner.

He saw a dark figure at the side of the road, and something in the middle of it—a bough of a tree. He jammed on his brakes, and was thrown forward, bumping his head on the windscreen. The car hit the bough; one front wheel mounted it, the other wouldn't take it, and the car slewed round. It crashed into the hedge, throwing Snub heavily against the door. Before he could recover, the other door opened and a man stretched out a hand and struck him viciously in the face. Then the fellow grabbed him by the neck and arm, and dragged him out of the car.

.   .   .   .   .

Jolly was even more distressed than he had shown to George or Snub. It was true that George's change of attitude had softened his manner towards the younger man, but it had not eased his anxiety. He knew that the obvious and right thing was to tell the police, and he couldn't withdraw from that now, but—it might do harm to Rollison. Not only that, but Rollison might be against this step.

He decided to go to Gresham Terrace before visiting Scotland Yard. It was just possible that he would find Rollison there, and Rollison would find a way of quieting Grice's suspicions. By then, Jolly regretted his telephone call, and he caught a bus to Piccadilly, paying very little attention to what went on about him.

As he approached the house in Gresham Terrace, he saw a dilapidated Ford standing outside. One of the square-bodied, high-chassis models, it was almost fit to take part in the London-to-Brighton old crocks' race.

A burly man sat at the wheel.

Jolly recognized the car, and his heart missed a beat.

He drew level with it.

"Well, blow me!" exclaimed the driver, a big, fat man with one cauliflower ear and massive fists. He squeezed out of the car, and, to Jolly's embarrassment, seized his hand and pumped it vigorously. "Well, blow *me*, Mr. Jolly, I am glad to see you! Come to see Mr. Ar," he added, and breathed wheezily down Jolly's neck.

"Mr. Rollison is extremely busy," said Jolly, "and I'm not sure that he's in."

"He ain't," said Ebbutt. "I've been up four times. No answer. And I got to get back, Jolly, got a promising boy for the light-weight class. But you'll do to take a message, Jolly."

"Gladly," said Jolly.

Bill Ebbutt, who was not only a retired heavy-weight but also a retired publican, liked to call himself a friend of the Toff; and it was true that Rollison called himself a friend of Bill Ebbutt's. Ebbutt had a gymnasium in the Mile End Road, and was always discovering boxers who packed a remarkable punch—and it was said that more champions came out of Ebbutt's stable than out of any other in London.

Ebbutt, moreover, was in touch with a remarkable variety of characters in the East End. He was a friend of the down-and-outs, an adviser of the unfortunates who had slipped from grace and seen the inside of one of Her Majesty's prisons. And he had often acted as Rollison's contact-man east of Aldgate Pump.

"Well, that's fine," said Ebbutt, grinning and showing his few discoloured teeth. "It's like this, Mr. Jolly. Mr. Ar was dahn our way last week. You know what's been up, don't yer? Some of the bad boys been 'aving a spot o' bother, pushed out on jobs they never wanted to do, and 'ave to give someone a rake-off."

Jolly said quietly, "Yes, Mr. Ebbutt." So Ebbutt had come about this business of Old Harry.

"There's bin more trouble," went on Ebbutt earnestly. "Mr. Ar arst me to let 'im know. Four more jobs was done last night—yer've seen the papers, 'aven't yer? And there was that job the night before last, when the girl was done in. I think that was one o' the same lot, an' I don't mind telling yer, I'm worried, Mr. Jolly. What I came to tell Mr. Ar was this: we're right be'ind him. Anyfink 'e wants doing, we'll fix it."

"I'll tell him," promised Jolly. "I'm afraid that I won't be able to deliver the message just yet, Mr. Ebbutt. Mr. Rollison has been out on this—ah—job, and he has been missing for twenty-four hours. I am rather worried."

"Strewth!" exclaimed Ebbutt. "Missin'!"

"I am sure that he will appear again before long," went on Jolly, "but if he is absent longer than I expect, then I may call on you. I have already informed the police."

"Oh," said Ebbutt, " 'ave yer? I dunno that I should 'a' done that, Mr. Jolly. Never 'ad much time for the narks meself, but yer know best. Tell yer wot—I'll spread the news arahnd, an' if there's anyone got any ideas where Mr. Ar is, I'll find aht. I'll let yer know."

"I'm sure you will, Mr. Ebbutt."

"Better get cracking," said Ebbutt. He let in the clutch,

waved, and drove off; the Ford rattled and snorted into the
gathering darkness towards Piccadilly. Jolly watched it out
of sight. He was relieved that Ebbutt knew about the
situation—at heart, he felt that he should have told him before telling the police. Rollison almost certainly would have
done so, and yet . . .

Jolly sighed, and went up to the flat.

He opened the door, and groped for the light switch.

He felt two hands clutch his throat and two thumbs press
against his windpipe. He had no chance to call out, no
chance to struggle.

  . . . . .

Snub sat, tied to a chair, under a glaring light which hurt
his eyes and made his head ache unbearably. He could see
the face of the man in front of him, a hard, ugly face with
pale-grey, glittering eyes. The man held a short piece of
rubber hose, and kept waving it in front of his face. He
strained against the cords which bound him, but knew that
he couldn't get free.

The questions were all the same.

How much did he know about what Rollison was doing?

He had tried to avoid answering, but couldn't last out.
He told the whole story—or, rather, it was dragged out of
him by the questioner. Whenever he hesitated, the rubber
cracked across his head. He hated himself for having told
even a part of the truth, but he had no choice; he thought
that Rollison would understand.

At last they untied him. He couldn't walk out of the
room by himself, two men had to help him away.

  . . . . .

They did not treat Jolly that way. They shut him up with
George for a quarter of an hour, and George told him of
Rollison's condition. Next they took him to a small room,
and stood him by the side of a window made of toughened
glass. He could see Rollison sitting in the armchair in the
big room, the theatre, staring blankly in front of him.

The squat man who talked to Jolly said: "Sure, he's blind. He'll stay that way, if you don't talk. To make sure of it, I'll use a red-hot poker, Jolly. I shouldn't wait long, if I were you."

Jolly did not wait long.

.   .   .   .   .

The news spread swiftly through the East End. It was whispered in dockside pubs and coffee-shops, in billiards halls and bowling alleys. It was the chief subject of conversation in Bill's gymnasium, even distracting attention from the performance of Bill's latest white hope. It reached the ears of many beat policemen, reached Divisional H.Q. and was passed on to Scotland Yard; any news about Rollison was considered worth reporting.

There was something else which spread on rumour's wings through the East End of London—for the first time there was open talk of the fact that many cracksmen and others were being blackmailed into working for 'them'— or for Old Harry. For the first time this story also reached the ears of the police, through the good offices of Willie the Nark, and that in turn was passed on to Scotland Yard.

It reached the ears of Superintendent Grice.

By then, Grice had grown tired of waiting for Jolly's promised call, and had visited the Gresham Terrace flat, finding no one in.

He had also been to Pelham Mews, where Armitage's flat was empty.

He knew nothing of Mr. Harry Webb, or the offices in Raffety House, but he had heard another rumour—this time from Fleet Street—that Rollison had been interested in George Armitage because of his Pools win. Grice was always prepared to listen to rumours, and on occasion had been known to act on one. This latest did not sound like Rollison, however.

About nine o'clock that night Grice left his Victoria flat and went to the *Old Rum Inn*, a small public house in a narrow turning near Fleet Street, where reporters and editors foregathered, and where he might pick up a great deal more information than he read in the newspapers.

Two or three men of the Street greeted Grice boisterously, recognizing his tall, spare figure, his rather sallow skin, stretched very tightly across his nose, where the bridge showed white. He had an ugly red scar on one temple, and he was dressed as usual in a brown suit.

He was pushed towards the bar, and bitter was placed in front of him. He noticed that there were more people than usual here for this time of night; that suggested that one of those present had a story and the others hoped they might pick up something about it.

In one corner a very tall man with a mop of grizzled hair was gesticulating wildly to a small group of people, which included a plump girl. She had glistening eyes, ripe red lips and ruffled hair. Every now and again the tall man called her Clara.

"Now what's all this about Rollison, Gricey?" asked one of the reporters who had greeted Grice. "Any truth in it?"

"I wouldn't be surprised," said Grice. "You know what he is."

"Question is, do *you*?" demanded the reporter, and there was a guffaw of laughter.

"I know what crazy stunts he gets up to," said Grice, "and I gather that his man's a bit worried because he's been out on his own, but—well, that's like Rollison. It wouldn't surprise me if he turned up here and asked me what I'd have." Grice drained his glass.

"What'll you have?" demanded the reporter, and guffawed.

"Same, thanks," said Grice.

"After something about Rollison?" asked a dark little man on the *Express*.

"I've heard so many rumours, I'd like to find out what's behind 'em," said Grice.

"Get over to the other corner," advised the dark little

man. "Fuzz-Wuzz thinks Clara Mickle picked up something from Rollison the other day—she met him at George Armitage's place. You know, the Pools winner."

"Anything about the Brayling job?" asked the little dark man casually. "They've sent for you, haven't they?"

"Yes. But there's nothing," said Grice. "I only wish there were. Not even off the record," he added, grinning. "That Lagonda vanished. You know what a slow job it is checking on cars, even of that make. We'll pick something up before long. Ah, thanks." He picked up the second glass, and moved towards Clara Mickle and the reporter nicknamed Fuzz-Wuzz.

Clara was doubled up with laughter; she was obviously nearly tight. There was a double whisky in her hand, and she tossed it off, laughed, and handed Fuzz-Wuzz her glass.

"Same again," she said. "Oh, Fuzzy, *wouldn't* you like to know! Poor old Fuzz! It's cost him a couple of quid to find out what Rollison told me, and he thinks I'll open up. Not me—I'm Clara the Clam."

Fuzz-Wuzz obtained another double, squirted in a little soda, handed it to her, and said: "Hang it, Clara, can't I buy you a few drinks without being accused of ulterior motives?"

"No," said Clara. "Some could, but you couldn't. Oh no! And," she giggled, "it's all a waste of time and money, but if only you knew what *I* know!"

"Drink up," urged Fuzz-Wuzz. "Plenty more to come."

"Oh no, not this little girl," said Clara. "I know when I've had enough. I'm going to sip this one, and then I'm going home to my lonely little bed. Anyone want to know my number? It's Abbey 03241. Ab—Ab—Abbey 0-3-2-4-1!" she crooned. Ab—Ab—Abbey 0-3-2-4-1! Ab—Ab—Abbey . . ."

She didn't leave the *Old Rum Inn* until closing-time, but she hadn't told Fuzz-Wuzz or anyone else what she knew. Fuzz-Wuzz said that he wanted to see her home, she wasn't fit to walk; but she refused the offer and left the inn. She walked steadily enough, although with great and exaggerated care. She caught a number 11 bus from Fleet Street and booked to Victoria Station. She alighted half-way along Victoria Street.

So did Grice.

So did a little man, who walked rapidly in front of Clara, whose gait was now unsteady. The little man took a turning to the right, and Clara and Grice followed him, although Grice was not thinking of the little man, only of the girl. It seemed certain that Rollison, for some reason or other, had confided in Clara Mickle. Grice felt sure that she would tell him why, but he wanted to make the inquiry informal; he had no wish to force an issue with any member of the Press.

Clara walked quickly along the narrow pavement of a street which was lighted only by the reflected light from the main road. Grice couldn't see her clearly, although he could hear her footsteps ringing out. She turned into the gateway leading to a block of flats, tall and gaunt against the night sky. There was hardly a glimmer of light here.

Clara hiccoughed loudly.

Next moment she uttered a half-scream, which broke off short. Grice heard a thud. He caught a glimpse of two struggling figures and rushed forward, snatching his torch from his pocket. The beam flashed out. He saw Clara, the little man and a knife which glittered evilly in the bright light. Clara was leaning back; the man clutched her hair from behind and stretched her neck, as if he were going to gash it. Grice hurled himself forward. The knife flashed again, cut; blood gushed.

Grice hit the little man a terrific blow on the side of the head, and the man knocked his head on the railings. Grice shouted: "*Police! Police!*" He wanted to help the girl, who had collapsed and was groaning, but he wanted desperately to make sure that her assailant didn't get away.

"*Police!*"

A door opened and a man called:

"What's up?"

"Come and hold this man!" Grice gasped, glancing up. He saw a woman behind the man in the doorway. "Telephone for a doctor, Hurry!"

.   .   .   .   .

The *Echo* had easily the best story. Its headlines screamed:

GIRL REPORTER SAVAGELY ATTACKED

TOFF BELIEVED KIDNAPPED

But most of the other dailies treated the affair as the big sensation of the morning. In most of the newspapers the attempted murder was linked up with Armitage and his pools winnings. There were many wild guesses and a number of shrewd ones.

By the evening, the Press was almost unanimous in its headlines—the Toff featured in them all. Photographs of Clara, Rollison, Jolly, Snub and Armitage decorated every paper. There were highly coloured accounts of Rollison's past activities, of his defiance of the police, of his friendship with many crooks in the East End. Relatives of the Toff, who were not only jealous of his good name, but always touchy where his investigations were concerned, had an extremely bad day. Anyone even remotely connected with him was telephoned; reporters as well as police watched the flat, Snub's rooms—which were not far away—and Pelham Mews.

But no newspaper and no policeman connected this mystery with the murder of the girl in the lonely house at Brayling. None mentioned Anne Meriton or Philip Rowse—and there was no reason known why they should—and none mentioned Mr. Harry Webb or Baxter.

During the morning the swarthy little man, whose name was Paul Lee, was charged with wounding with intent to murder Clara Mickle. Only evidence of arrest was given, and he was remanded for eight days. He had not uttered a word of explanation, although he must have known that if the girl died he would receive no mercy. After the court hearing he withstood two hours of police questioning, and was submitted to another intensive interrogation during the afternoon, but still refused to speak.

By that time Grice had collected a great deal of information, and reported in full to the Assistant Commissioner. The fact that Rollison had obviously been working on a case without the knowledge of the police hardly mattered now.

"As I see it, sir," Grice said to the tall, grey-haired Assistant Commissioner, who respected the superintendent very much indeed, "Rollison must have uncovered, or come near to uncovering, something very big. Nothing else would explain this wholesale kidnapping. As I've pointed out, Jolly was undoubtedly kidnapped; if they'd just wanted him dead they would have killed him at the flat. Whoever is behind it has made a clean sweep—and I don't mind admitting I wish I could have five minutes with Rollison. He can usually see through a brick wall."

"You'll find him," said the Assistant Commissioner.

"I'm beginning to wonder," said Grice. "He's been missing for two days now. And if he can't help himself, I'm not a bit sure that anyone else can help him."

"How's Clara Mickle?" asked the A.C.

"Danger-list," said Grice briefly. "Touch and go."

CHAPTER XIV

BLIND MAN'S BLUFF

ROLLISON woke up with a start and lay back, recalling what had happened.

He had spoken to George, a horrified, angry, inarticulate George. To Snub, also inarticulate, numbed by what he had discovered. And to Jolly. After the first moment of understanding, when Rollison had been able to imagine his expression, Jolly had been—just Jolly. Quiet, undramatic, refusing to believe that there was even a risk of permanency in the blindness. "Why, sir, the man here actually said that he would make it permanent if I refused to give him what little information I could. Consequently, I told him, sir."

"Yes," Rollison had said. "Quite right."

"I'll say it's right." The harsh-voiced man had spoken, and Jolly had been taken away, leaving Rollison with a suspicion that his man would like to pass on other news.

So all three were here, or had been here; he knew of no reason why they should be taken away. The danger was that they might be murdered, but—would *any* man commit wholesale slaughter? Wasn't their captor more likely to keep them here until he had finished his foul work, whatever that work might be, and was safely out of the country?

Anne Meriton was here too.

Calm, composed, frightened Anne.

He had heard from George and Snub how she had telephoned George and afterwards come with him. George had turned against her, bitterly.

Now . . .

Rollison wished he knew what had awakened him. The misty darkness was infuriating, frustrating; he did not even know whether it was night or day.

But he mustn't dwell too much on the unnatural darkness, it was only important in so far as it affected the crimes. And he had to admit that he didn't know a great deal about them, beyond the basic fact that 'they'—and the harsh-voiced man was doubtless one of their leaders—were exerting pressure to compel practised criminals to work for them.

There had been many big robberies during the past month. Probably £20,000 had been stolen—or goods worth at least that sum. There were big pickings, and yet—two things made Rollison doubt whether the organizers were quite so efficient as they appeared to be, and also whether they were simply cashing-in on criminals.

They had used George Armitage.

Why?

There were many expert drivers who would have done the job that George had been forced to do, and thought nothing of it. Twenty-five or fifty pounds would have paid them well; they would have been fully satisfied, and certainly would not have told the police or the Toff anything about what they had done.

Yet 'they' had used George, knowing that in his frame of mind he was capable of doing all manner of wild things. And, of course, they had tried to shut his mouth by murder. They'd been quick to see the danger, and yet—the would-be murderer's gun had been loaded with blanks. Just a mistake? He could hardly believe that.

When he examined the facts about George he was forced to one conclusion. That someone had been deliberately forcing George into this corner—encouraged him in his gambling, created the situation whereby he had been reduced to his present plight. He was still alive; they could have killed him *en route*, there was no need for them to keep him alive. Yet the harsh-voiced man had said that 'they could use a man with money', although George with money was even more likely to talk than George without, because he wasn't so completely helpless. It didn't add up. And to have used George on the Brayling job certainly hadn't the hall-mark of efficiency.

The thing which made Rollison wonder whether they were just cashing-in on a new kind of racket—new, that was, for England—was as simple. Would 'they' have taken the risk of kidnapping him, Jolly, George and Snub if that was all they were doing? Murder wasn't a crime which any-one committed if it could possibly be avoided. The murder of the maid was understandable—she had come upon the thieves unexpectedly, and they'd killed her in a moment of madness—but the attempt on George came into a different category; so did the kidnappings.

One fact stood out clearly in Rollison's mind: 'They' could not safely release any one of the prisoners.

Rollison turned over in bed. He was wide-awake now, whether it were two o'clock or ten o'clock in the morning. He wasn't particularly hungry, although he had been given only a little bread and water the previous night.

Supposing it *was* night?

Would they guard his room? Or would they assume that he could do nothing, and leave him unguarded?

If only this misty darkness——

There he was, back again at the personal angle, danger-ously near self-pity. He mustn't allow that; once he sub-mitted to it, he would be like clay in 'their' hands. He must forget the darkness, the mist, and——

He went rigid.

Mist!

There had been none yesterday or the day before. Then there had been only blackness. Now it was as if he were looking at dark grey smoke—not moving smoke, more like a pall of fog, a good old London pea-souper.

He sat up slowly and stared straight in front of him. Yes, there it was, this pall. He turned his head slowly to-wards the right; it was exactly the same. He looked towards the left—and caught his breath again, and gripped the sides of the bed so tensely that it hurt. He looked round, then back towards the left. It wasn't imagination, the 'smoke' was lighter in that direction, darker whenever he looked elsewhere. He pushed back the bedclothes, climbed out of the double bed on the left-hand side, and groped forward, with his hands outstretched. He touched fabric, probably a curtain; he touched glass, and proved that he was at the window. He stared into a grey mist, and he knew that sight was gradually percolating back; he was no longer stone-blind.

Now his heart hammered as he held on to the curtains for support. His sudden weakness was partly due to lack of food, of course; the discovery would not have affected him so much had he not been hungry, but—he *could* see a little. He might soon be able to make out shapes.

Did 'they' know that the complete blindness would last only for a few days?

Or—could he bluff them while his sight came back?

He began to smile—and had Jolly or Snub seen him they would have known that the feeling of utter helplessness had gone.

He heard a sound behind him, a handle turning. He heard a stifled gasp, as if someone were surprised to see him standing there, and he guessed it was—*Anne*.

He said, "Good morning."

"*Hush!*" It was an agonized whisper. "I want to help."

"You haven't shown much inclination yet," said Rollison dryly.

"I couldn't help myself," she said, "I've been forced—but never mind that. I've brought you some food. Sit down. Sit down!" she repeated impatiently, as if she had forgotten that he couldn't see. Then she said, "Oh, I'm sorry; I'll lead you." She took his hand; hers was very cold. She led him to the bed, and he sat down. She took his legs and swung them on to the bed, and then punched the pillows behind him, so that he could sit up in comfort. Then she took his hand again, and put something in it—a roll, soft and new.

"What time is it?" asked Rollison.

"Half past seven. You haven't long. Hurry."

"Don't forget the risk of indigestion," said Rollison. That was an inane remark, one he regretted as soon as it was out of his mouth. The weakness, of course—and the over-whelming fact that food was in his hand. He bit into the roll. It wasn't just bread, there was soft meat in it; chicken. He mustn't gobble, indigestion was no joke and he would get a severe attack if he ate too quickly after nearly three days without food.

He finished it while Anne stood by the bedside, presumably looking down at him. He couldn't discern even the vaguest outline of her figure, but there was still grey 'smoke', not utter darkness.

"Here's another," she said, putting it into his hand.

"Thanks. How did you manage to get in here?"

"I know they're not about much before eight o'clock," she said. "There's a man on duty in the hall and another on the landing, but—well, I managed to slip past them. They get careless after dawn breaks, they don't think there's anything to worry about. I told the cook the rolls were for me."

"You're quite popular in this household, aren't you?" mumbled Rollison.

"Oh, please don't sneer at me! I've tried hard to do the right thing."

"Well, possibly," said Rollison. He judged her position, moved his hand, and touched hers. He caught it in a firm grip, and although she tried to free herself, he wouldn't let her go. He looked up, believing her face to be very close to his; and he smiled grimly, mirthlessly. "Anne, what's it all about?" he demanded.

"Never mind *that*," she whispered, "I want to help you to get away."

"Oh, no," said Rollison, and there was a confident note in his voice; the pressure of his lean, brown fingers grew stronger. "When I'm ready to go, I'll go; you're not going to help me, Anne."

"Don't be silly! You can't get away without help."

"That's where you and I disagree," said Rollison.

Bluff.

It was quite possible that the man with the harsh voice had sent her here, to learn what she could from him. It would do no harm for her to report that he seemed sure that he could get away whenever he wanted to. Blind man's bluff!

"What—what do you mean?" she whispered.

Rollison smiled, and this time there was humour in his expression. Although he did not know it, his eyes were dilated, but there was a grey fringe, and the smile was enough to make her catch her breath.

"Your boy friend doesn't know everything," he said, "and I can get away when I want to, Anne, but—I want to know why you're here, what you mean by saying you've tried to act for the best. They're blackmailing you—is that it?"

"I—yes. Yes, but——"

"Black past? Or are they turning the screw because they've someone near and dear to you in their power?" asked Rollison. He made the words sound almost facetious, but they held an underlying note of seriousness which she couldn't fail to notice.

"I—I've done nothing. I *hadn't* done anything, but a friend——"

"Ah! In love?" murmured Rollison.

"No! No, it isn't that, it—*hush*."

She broke off, and Rollison strained his ears to catch the sound which made her stop. It came from outside. Someone was walking briskly on gravel—up the drive along a path leading past the house. The footsteps drew nearer and louder, and then fainter.

"It—it's all right," she muttered, "I think it's the milkman. Or the postman."

"Where are we?" asked Rollison.

"I don't know the district at all," said Anne, "I'm not

even allowed in the grounds on my own. Mr. Rollison, *can* you escape?"

"Oh, yes."

"Then why——"

"In my own good time," said Rollison cheerfully. "You haven't another of those rolls, I suppose? Ah, thanks!" The third tasted as good as the first. "While I'm here I'm going to find out what it's all about," he went on. "It would really be a help if you'll tell me about your part. You're being blackmailed because of—well, shall we say an old man with a bald head and a beard?"

Anne cried, "How did you *know*?"

"*Hush!*" hissed Rollison, and finished his roll. He had remembered Snub's story of the old man whom she had kissed good night—and the shot in the dark had hit the target. He smiled at her.

"Isn't it enough that I do know?" he asked.

"I don't understand—oh, never mind! Yes, he's in great danger—grave danger—and he's been so good to me, I just had to help him." She began to speak very quickly. "I didn't understand what I was doing at first, but—*he's* being blackmailed."

"Is he rich?"

"Oh yes, he's almost a millionaire," she said, so quickly that it sounded casual. "And these people——"

"Who *are* these people?"

"I don't know their names, but there's one man here, I've heard him called Luke. Just Luke. And there's Baxter and Old Harry; but they're not important, Luke tells me what to do. You see, Uncle——"

"Your uncle?"

"Actually, I'm no relation," said Anne, "but I've always called him Uncle—he was a great friend of my father. Oh, *that* doesn't matter. He was being blackmailed, and was terribly worried. You—your man Snub knows by whom."

"*Does* he, then," murmured Rollison. "Rowse?"

"Yes," said Anne, and went on very quickly. "Please

don't interrupt, I want to tell you now, but there isn't much time. It all began when men visited my uncle some time ago—Luke, a man named Webb, and Philip Rowse. I didn't like them; I thought Uncle was worried by them, and made him tell me the truth. They were blackmailing him. Lately, he's always paid Rowse; the other men stopped coming. So I struck up an acquaintance with Rowse; that wasn't difficult. You see, I thought he had some papers, something—I don't know what—about my uncle, and I wanted to get them back. It seemed easy enough, and—well, Rowse fell in love with me."

She paused: Rollison did not speak.

"And then *he* told me that he was being blackmailed," Anne went on, in a helpless voice. "At first I didn't believe him—I didn't say so, but I thought he suspected what I was after, and was trying to defend himself, but I'm sure that isn't true. He didn't have to pay money—he had to collect money from my uncle and, he said, from others. He got a commission—ten per cent of everything he collected. He just couldn't help himself, and—and I believed him."

"I *see*," murmured Rollison. "How did you come to know Baxter and these other people?"

"Through Philip Rowse."

"And is *Rowse* trying to clear himself, too?" asked Rollison.

"No, he—he said that there was nothing he could do, that he would have to go on obeying his orders until they——"

"They?"

"I only know them as that," said Anne. "Philip's never named them. I'm not even sure whether he knows them or not. Anyhow, he's reconciled to the position. I told him nothing about what I was doing, but I thought I might find out more from him. My uncle agreed that was wise——"

"So your uncle knows what you're doing, does he?" remarked Rollison.

"Yes, I told him—he was against it at first, but he's old and rather frail, and he couldn't stop me."

"Wilful young woman," murmured Rollison. "And now you've found yourself in the clutches of these gentry. They've discovered what you're doing, and threaten dire consequences to your adopted uncle if you don't obey. Is that right?"

"Yes. Yes, and now——"

"No time for remorse or regrets," said Rollison. "Who owns that Lagonda, Anne?"

Anne said: "Philip. It's one of several; he doesn't use the Lagonda much."

"Why didn't you tell me before?" demanded Rollison.

"I didn't want to betray him, I think—I think he *is* trying to do his best. And he once told me that they borrow one of his cars sometimes. That night they may have taken it, but I don't *know* that they did."

"I see," said Rollison gently. "Anne, if you're telling me the truth, you've one big fault. You're far too loyal to people who aren't worth it. But let's think about the present situation. You mustn't risk getting yourself in bad with Luke. I don't like Luke. Just do as you're told, until I tell you differently. And before you go, one other thing. Have you any reason to believe that they've a special reason for getting their claws into George?"

"George Armitage?"

"Yes."

"No, I——" began Anne.

But she didn't go on, for Rollison heard footsteps outside in the passage.

They stopped at the door.

CHAPTER XV

COMPANY FOR THE TOFF

ANNE drew in a sharp, hissing breath—evidence, if more were needed, that she was really frightened of being discovered. Her hand brushed Rollison's.

"Baxter?" That was Luke's voice in the passage.

"Yeh?" Baxter called back.

There were more footsteps; Luke was approaching the door now. The handle turned but the door did not open.

Anne whispered desperately: "I'll try to climb out of the window. Don't—don't," she repeated in anguish, for Rollison caught her hand again. "I must go, it isn't a high window."

"Get in the bed," ordered Rollison softly. "Come on, hurry." Baxter and Luke were talking just outside the door, keeping their voices low, so that Rollison could not hear what they were saying. "Pull the clothes over you—*hurry.*"

There was a pause. Luke was talking.

Rollison felt the bedclothes move; Anne's slim legs brushed against his; she slid down. He could feel her pulling the clothes over her. She was on the side near the window, away from the door. He suddenly remembered the rolls, and lifted the sheet and blanket.

"Any food left?"

"No," came her muffled answer.

"Don't worry," said Rollison. "I'm going to raise my knees, so get as far under them as you can, and keep still."

She did so; he felt her hair brush against his leg, where the pyjama-trousers were caught up near his knees. He didn't speak again, but smoothed out the bedclothes and ran his hand along the side, to make sure that no part of the girl was showing. Now the frustrating helplessness of being unable to see made him wildly angry; it was at least possible that whoever came in would see at a glance that——

He grinned, in spite of himself.

He held one arm beneath the sheet, making a tunnel so that the air could get down to her—and then the door opened and a man stepped into the room. It was Luke; he knew that before the man spoke, for Baxter had a heavy deliberate tread, this was lighter. Luke closed the door quietly and came towards him, and Rollison's smile faded.

"Well, Rollison," said Luke. "Decided to tell me everything yet?"

"I have told you everything I can," said Rollison patiently, "and if you want it repeated—I know there is blackmail on a large and unusual scale. I tried to find out who was behind it, and got no further than Baxter, and talk of Old Harry. I have not consulted the police."

Luke chuckled.

"I almost believe you, Rollison. That's exactly the same as Jolly and Higginbottom have told me, and I don't believe three people would make the same statement without some differences if it weren't true. But—look at what you've left *out*." He was very close to the bed now.

"Meaning?" inquired Rollison, and stifled a yawn.

"What did you tell that woman reporter?"

"Woman——" began Rollison, and then realized that Luke was talking of Clara. "Well, well," he said, "you do get around. How did you know that I'd told her anything?"

"It's the talk of Fleet Street," said Luke, "and I don't want any more lies from you."

"Do you mean that Clara didn't keep it to herself?" demanded Rollison. He chuckled. "I've sold a pup to the whole Street, have I? They'll never forgive me."

Luke slapped him across the face.

Rollison jerked his hand up, touched the other's, tried to grab his wrist, but failed. All his good intentions faded, and he said harshly: "That's enough thuggery, damn you!

I've taken all I'm going to take from you; if you touch me again I'll smash your face in."

He sensed that Luke backed away in surprised alarm.

"And don't imagine I can't do it just because I can't see you," went on Rollison harshly. "You and I are alone in the room, and I would break your neck once I got hold of you. You've asked for the truth. I'll give it to you. But if you try any more rough stuff you won't get another word out of me."

After a long pause, Luke said: "Tell me about Clara, Rollison."

"All right. She hung around the day that I was talking to George, and discovered that I was working on a job. I fobbed her off by saying that I was trying to find out who was rooking the pool prize-winners right and left, and asked her to keep it to herself until her paper comes out—she's on the *Sunday Letter*. I thought she would keep it to herself," he added, leaning back. His knees lowered, his calf pressed into Anne's neck. He raised it quickly, and felt her move.

"Oh, she tried," said Luke.

"What do you mean, tried?"

Luke came nearer, and touched his arm.

"Rollison, don't fly off the handle at me again, and don't try any rough stuff yourself, or you'll wish you'd never been born," he warned. "Clara boasted that you'd told her plenty, but she didn't say what it was. Other Press men tried to get her drunk, but she still didn't talk. And then— I made sure she couldn't talk. Understand?" His voice was thick with rage. "I made sure she couldn't—I wiped her out, see. The whole story's here—the whole story, and you can't read it. Try—try, Rollison!" He snatched his hand away and pressed something close to Rollison's face; a paper; there was a faint smell of printer's ink from it. "Go on, *read*!" shrieked Luke. "Open your eyes, you poor blind fool, and read!" He snatched the paper away and struck Rollison over the head with it; the paper tore. "I'll teach you to get rough with me!"

Rollison didn't move.

"Now, let's have the *whole* truth," said Luke. He took Rollison's wrist. "Get up. Come on, get up?"

He pulled; Anne wriggled. Rollison leaned back, using all his weight, although he knew he couldn't really defend himself, couldn't stop himself from being dragged out of bed.

And then someone shouted outside.

A shot rang out.

Luke's grip eased; he stared towards the window. Another shot was followed by running footsteps. Baxter yelled something.

Luke swung round and sprang towards the door.

.   .   .   .   .

Rollison couldn't see Anne's red face, tousled hair and bright eyes as she popped her head out of the bed-clothes. She scrambled off the bed, breathing very heavily. Rollison leaned back, tense, fearful because of what was happening outside. One emergency gone, another here—and this was probably the worse. Obviously one of the prisoners had made a bid for escape, and the hunt was up. He stared towards the grey mist of the window, and the newspaper rustled as it fell from the bed to the floor.

He said: "Be careful, Anne. Don't let them see you, but tell me what's happening outside."

"It—it's your friend, Higginbottom. He's at the end of the garden, three men—no, four men—are after him. Baxter—Baxter has a gun."

The picture was vivid; he felt as if he could see every movement—Snub's lithe, lean figure, speeding on the wings of great courage, looking round perhaps, aware that any moment might be his last.

"Has he a chance?" Rollison asked softly.

"There's a copse—at the end of the garden," Anne said. "If he reaches that he might——"

She broke off; another shot rang out.

"Got him?" asked Rollison.

"No, he's still running . . . he's only twenty yards from the trees now . . . two of them are running across the lawn, to try to cut him off . . . oh, he'll make it, he must make it now!" Anne caught her breath; Rollison clutched the sides of the bed and stared towards her. "He's near there . . . oh, he's fallen!"

Rollison swore beneath his breath.

"He's getting up," Anne said tensely. "Baxter's still a long way off; he'll make it, he—oh, he's down again!"

"He's hit," said Rollison flatly.

Anne didn't speak.

"Have they——" began Rollison.

"Yes," said Anne in a dull voice. "Baxter's caught him." She turned round and came to the bed. "Mr. Rollison, I'm the only one who can get away. I must try—I must bring help. I can't help what happens to me. I can't allow all of you to stay here, they might murder you. I must try."

Rollison said, "Lie low for a bit, Anne."

But he couldn't bring himself to argue with her. He still stared sightlessly towards the window. He heard footsteps on the drive and could picture them carrying or dragging Snub back to the house.

.   .   .   .   .

"Yes," said Rollison at last, "lie low for a bit, Anne, there'll be a chance of doing something soon, but not yet. If you can sneak in with some food now and again, you'll be doing all you can. Have you a key?"

"Yes, I took one from the outside of the door," said Anne. "There was a lot of trouble when they discovered that it was missing, but—well, does that matter?"

"We mustn't let it," said Rollison. "And you must go, they're so worked up because of Snub just now they won't notice you if you turn up suddenly."

He heard her gasp.

After a moment, he asked, "What is it, Anne?"

"It—I just caught sight of the headlines," said Anne.

"It's so wicked. If I'd dreamt what would happen I wouldn't——"

She read the story of the attack on Clara, the assailant's capture by Grice, in person, and the fact that Clara was still on the danger-list. He asked her to look at the stop press news, but there was only a paragraph about UNO in it, no further news about Clara. She dropped the paper on to the bed, and said: "I'd better go."

"And don't forget we're not finished yet," said Rollison, "not by a long, long way."

He heard the door close. He waited until he felt that she was safely away, and no one had noticed her leave the room. Had she been seen there would have been an uproar immediately. The sounds outside had faded. He had no idea how badly Snub was hurt; he could only hope for the best. He tried not to think too much about Snub, and turned his thoughts to Clara. And from Clara to Grice.

No wonder Luke had wanted to know what he had told Clara: for Clara might come round, and inform Grice. He had been so determined not to tell the police about this business yet; now it had been done for him. He wondered if he had convinced Luke. He had scared the man for a moment—that was an achievement, although he realized now that it had been a foolish move. Luke had him completely at his mercy, and in the wild temper which had seized him after the rebuff he might have done anything.

Rollison just could not anticipate any more. A man could draw a gun, or pull a knife from his pocket, without giving any warning. This helplessness!

But he felt much better; those rolls had been delicious. Now he wanted a cigarette. He groped for a chair which stood by the bedside; his jacket hung over the back.

He took out his cigarette-case and lighter, put a cigarette between his lips, and flicked the lighter. He held it about where he thought the end of the cigarette was.

He saw a glow.

CHAPTER XVI

PROPOSITION

ROLLISON held the lighter tightly. The glow remained, not bright but unmistakable. He got up and went slowly towards the window, feeling a soft breeze come in, and the warmth which had really been his first warning of what had happened to him. It was light-grey outside. He looked upwards—and saw a white ball in the middle of the greyness; like the moon behind wispy, diaphanous clouds. He knew that it was the sun.

He turned away, hearing someone approach.

The door opened, and he recognized Luke's tread.

Luke slammed the door and approached him, and Rollison would not have been surprised had he been struck. But Luke stopped a little way in front of him, and growled: "Higginbottom won't do much running about for a while."

"So Snub got out, did he?" murmured Rollison.

"He didn't get far. And if he or anyone else tries to get away again, I'll kill him," said Luke. The threat came out quite flatly; he meant it.

"Why don't you kill us all, and be done with it?" demanded Rollison.

"That would be the easy way out for you," said Luke in the same flat voice. "But you aren't going to find it so easy, Rollison. I can use you—you and Jolly, Arm——" He broke off abruptly. "You especially," he went on quickly. "They're very fond of you in the East End of London, Rollison, aren't they? *Very* fond. And they're getting a bit restive." A spring creaked; he was sitting down. "And I don't mind telling you——"

He stopped again.

Rollison hardly knew why this pause alarmed him, but it did.

Luke growled, "What's that paper doing there?"

The newspaper which Anne had read; it might give her away. Rollison looked towards the window.

"Over—there," said Luke. He stood up; little noises sounded very loud to Rollison, Luke probably thought he had made none. Next moment, Rollison saw something very dark in the grey mist. He didn't flinch; subconsciously he guessed what had happened, what Luke suspected. The shape moved swiftly, like a great dark shadow in front of his eyes; he blinked, but did not start back.

Luke said softly, "You can't *see*, Rollison, can you?"

Rollison said as softly, "If I could see you wouldn't be sitting there, I'd strangle the life out of you."

"Oh," said Luke. "Oh." He gave a little giggle—he had been convinced by the word 'sitting'. He moved away again and sat down. "All right, all right," he said, "I thought you'd been trying to read that paper. Listen, Rollison—I'm doing something in the East End which will make you and the police and your previous pals, the crooks, sit up. I'm going to organize the East End so that you wouldn't recognize it. The police won't know what's hit them."

"Ah," said Rollison. "So you're going to introduce business efficiency methods into Limehouse, are you?"

Luke said: "Sure—that's a good way to put it, Rollison. I'm going to get *more* experts taught. I'm going to organize crime as it's never been organized before. I'm going to plan the jobs. Find out where the stuff is ready for picking up. Get it all worked out, detail the men to their jobs, have one big clearing-house for everything. Fifty per cent to the man who does the job, fifty per cent to me, for organizing it. Like the idea?" he added abruptly.

"It's been tried before," said Rollison. "And failed."

"*This* won't fail," said Luke. "Half the jobs that have been done in the past two months were with my backing.

You see, I'm going to pay the boys when they're off duty. They'll be well looked after."

"Dole for thieves," murmured Rollison.

"Sure." Luke giggled again. "Dole for thieves—that's a good one. I can see you've got the idea. I've got the markets planned, too. Furs—there's a lot of money in furs, these days especially. I've got some of the export houses marked down. I'm breaking in the crooks. They don't like it much, but they've got to like it. They've got to realize that there'll be much more in it for them if they come into the syndicate than if they stay outside. Well, Rollison, what about *that*?"

"It's ambitious," conceded Rollison.

"It's good, Mr. Ruddy Toff!" Luke stood up again. "Listen to me. I've got a team of solicitors ready, a few mouthpieces too—any man who gets caught will be defended *free*, and he won't have to ask the court for legal aid, and get a doddering old fool, or a kid just out of college. I've got a shipping company lined up, to get stuff out of the country *and* to get stuff in. I'm going into this in a big way, Rollison, and—*you're* going to help."

"Thanks," murmured Rollison.

"You won't like it any more than the other fools like it now," went on Luke, "but it's going to happen my way. I know a lot about you. I know that most of the boys in the East End trust you. You're going to sell my idea to them. I'm going to use you and Jolly and——"

He nearly said 'Armitage' again; but just stopped himself. And Rollison tucked that fact away in his mind, while he tried to think objectively of what the man had said.

It was a great conception, although from a warped mind. He had to admit to himself that no one had ever tried to do this on such a scale, and—it *might* succeed for a time. The weakness of the criminal fraternity was their disunity. They worked in fits and starts, no man knew what the next was going to do. And in that lay the great strength of the police. But if organized robbery, crime of every kind, confronted the police it would have initial success because the police would have to alter their methods to tackle it.

"That's shaken you," gloated Luke.

"It would shake me if I thought you'd worked it out for yourself," said Rollison, "but it's too ambitious, you haven't the brains to think of it or carry it out. Who's the real big shot?" He wanted to anger Luke and thus perhaps make him speak more freely.

"Any more of that talk and I'll bash you," growled Luke.

"But my dear Luke, isn't it true?" another man asked.

Luke gave a startled exclamation and sprang to his feet. Rollison looked towards the door. Neither of them had heard the newcomer enter, but, judging from his voice, he was now on the threshold. Yes—there was a tiny click as the door closed. There were no other sounds, but when the newcomer spoke again he was much nearer.

"Don't look so shocked, my friend, you knew that I was coming this morning." He paused, advanced a little nearer, and went on: "So *this* is the great Rollison. Good morning, Mr. Rollison. I will say that I admire your spirit."

It was a soft and gentle voice, like that of an old man. It held a curious quality, as if he were amused, and smiling at his own secret source of amusement. In spite of that impression, Rollison did not like the voice, and he felt sure that he would always recognize it again.

"Aren't you going to return my greeting?" asked the man with the gentle voice. "But I forgot—you are a gentleman, and gentlemen like to be formally introduced. Luke, show Mr. Rollison how well brought up you've been."

Luke muttered; "I don't get——"

"Now come, Luke! Tell Mr. Rollison who I am."

"He needn't worry," said Rollison, leaning back and trying to look unconcerned. "I'll make a guess that you're no less than the gentleman called Old Harry."

"But how shrewd," purred the other. "Yes, I am Old Harry, and I thought it time that you and I had a chat,

Rollison. It was I who decided that you should be brought here, instead of being killed. Luke is rather crude in some of his methods, I'm afraid, and very objective—he felt that you were better dead; I felt that we might be able to work to our mutual advantage. Just a difference in approach, you see. Luke"—he turned to the other man, who had not yet recovered from his shock—"I'm not very pleased with what's happened here. When Higginbottom ran off you should have used air-guns or silenced automatics, those shots were heard half a mile away—I know, because I heard them myself."

"No one would guess——" began Luke hoarsely.

"Oh, but you can never tell what anyone might guess," said Old Harry. Menace crept into his voice, and Rollison judged that Luke was afraid of him; he could understand that. "Look how quickly Rollison guessed my identity. And there are tradesmen not far away, they might have seen something of what happened," went on Old Harry. "It was very careless to allow Higginbottom to get away. Who was responsible?"

"I don't know that——"

"Who was responsible?" barked Old Harry.

Luke muttered, "Baxter."

"This is the second time that Baxter has made a serious mistake," said Old Harry. "I will speak to him myself. Go and see that everything is all right now, Luke."

"It is, I made sure——"

"Go and make *quite* sure," ordered Old Harry. "And see that the girl is locked in her room. Where are you keeping her, by the way?"

"In the next room to this," said Luke.

"I am not at all sure that we can rely on her," said Old Harry. "Lock her away until I have gone, I don't want anyone to see me."

Luke said, "No one would recognize you in that get-up."

"Luke, I want to talk to Rollison—*alone*," said Old Harry.

Luke seemed reluctant to go, but he made no further pro-test. The door opened and closed. Rollison looked towards the other man and heard him move across the room—soft, stealthy movements.

"It is a lovely morning," said Old Harry. "Spring at its most glorious best, Rollison. The leaves are unfurling, and in the shrubbery just to the right of the house there is a wonderful display of daffodils, fully out now, a smiling, yellow carpet. Are you looking forward to the next few months?"

Rollison did not answer.

He knew that this man was deliberately taunting him about his blindness; that his description of the garden was calculated to have one effect—to make him long to be able to see outside. The gentle voice was not a reflection of a quiet spirit, here was a man capable of great cruelty.

"*Would* you look forward to them, if you could see?" asked Old Harry.

"I always look forward to the future, chiefly because one can never tell what's going to happen next," said Rollison.

Old Harry laughed.

"I always look forward to the future; I wonder who is going to help me next. I never thought that Rollison—the great Toff!—would work for me, but that just goes to prove the glorious uncertainty of life, doesn't it? Rollison, do you ever want to see again?"

Rollison let that question pass unanswered, too.

"I feel sure you do," said Old Harry. "As a matter of fact, Rollison, I used this particular weapon on you because I know its effectiveness. I fought—for freedom, King and country!—and I was blinded for a short while. For a month or two I suffered all the horrors of the damned, while the awful realization that I might never see again came over me. I am a strong-willed man, Rollison, like you—yet I became a nervous wreck. I didn't care what happened provided I could see again. I was prepared to sell my soul to the Devil."

"You have," murmured Rollison.

Old Harry laughed again.

"Yes, I have—but I didn't do it then. It was the wicked unconcern of the country for which I'd fought which made me change my allegiance, Rollison. Oh, the miracle happened and I regained my sight. I was discharged from hospital, fully cured, only to find that there was no place for me in civil life. Like thousands of others I drifted, purposeless. Then my wife died from cancer. I lived honestly, if you can say that I lived, until after she had died; then I decided that I had done with scruples, done with what you call honesty. I became a bad man, Rollison!

"Riches came almost at once, because I was clever and careful, qualities which availed me nothing in my law-abiding life, but were outstanding in a criminal career. Have you ever pondered over the ignorance, the low intellectual standard, of criminals? That's why they're so easily caught. A clever rogue is a rare creature, and a clever rogue nearly always outwits the police. But I'm sure you've thought of that, Rollison. The result of my thinking was very simple. I decided that I would live to see crime really organized. Luke's told you what I intend to do, I believe?"

"What you intend to try to do," corrected Rollison.

"I think it is rather more than that," said Old Harry. "In fact, Rollison, I have only one obstacle to overcome now—I want the trust of these people. The big and the little crooks, the creatures who are not particularly good or bad but are united in one thing—hatred of the police. But they are almost united in one other thing, Rollison—trust in *you*. I have made full inquiries and I congratulate you on having broken down the prejudice that they had against you in the first place. For a man of breeding and high position to win the confidence of the poor and the criminal is a remarkable achievement. Now you have an opportunity to turn it to your advantage."

Rollison said, "Oh!"

"Yes, a wonderful opportunity," purred Old Harry. "I

want you to persuade these people to trust *me*. If you
succeed, and I am sure that you can, then all will be well
and your sight will be restored. If you refuse, or if you fail
—well, then, Rollison, you will never see again. Your
present condition is temporary but I can easily make it
permanent. Would you like to consider that, and tell me
your decision when I come again?"

CHAPTER XVII

NIGHT

THERE had been a great change since Old Harry's visit.

They brought Rollison food—a belated breakfast, lunch, tea; it was now a little after half past seven, and nearly time for dinner. There had been few sounds in the house since Old Harry had left in a powerful car, which Rollison had heard purring down the drive. Luke had not been to see him; Anne had not come again.

Obviously, no one suspected that he was beginning to see. This filled him with a rising excitement which he rigidly controlled, but which made all the difference to his outlook. The horror of Old Harry's threat had not really touched him—because Old Harry didn't know the truth. Rollison did not greatly care *why* his sight was returning, his one concern was in case he should suffer a relapse. Throughout the day he had tested his vision every hour—with the striking of a clock outside. And every hour it had improved a little. Possibly he had not been given a strong dose of the drug; or else he had resisted it more than most.

He sat waiting; planning.

He heard footsteps at long last, and they stopped outside his door. Baxter and another man came in with a tray. Baxter, who sounded subdued, led him to a chair, and put a spoon and fork in his hands, told him that the food was cut up, and left him to eat succulent roast beef, roast potatoes, greens, with apple charlotte and dairy cream to follow.

When a man came to clear away, Rollison said:

"What time is it?"

"Neely nine," said the man, and didn't speak again.

Nearly nine o'clock.

He waited for what he judged to be two hours. There was

quiet everywhere now, the soft country sounds of the day had faded. He stubbed out a cigarette in an ashtray by the side of the bed, and went to the door. His heart began to thump. He tried the handle, but the door was locked. He took a nail file from his pocket and bent it at the thin end, pushed this into the keyhole and twisted and turned. The faint noise of metal on metal sounded very loud. With the tool in his knife, he could have opened this door in a few seconds, but they had removed his knife and it would take much longer than that with this improvised instrument; he might even fail. He did not lose patience, but kept on working in the utter darkness—until suddenly the hooked end caught the barrel of the lock. He pressed very gently, hardly daring to breathe.

The barrel moved.

He maintained the pressure, afraid that the file would slip again.

There was a clink!—and the lock went back.

His heart thumped so loudly now that he could hardly bear to stand there, gripping the handle. He did so, waiting until he was breathing more normally and could listen to anything that happened outside. The house was so quiet that he hoped everyone had gone to bed. It must now be half past eleven.

He opened the door.

Someone downstairs said: "Okay—keep your eyes skinned. Jolly *might* try to get away."

"Not on your life," said another man.

Rollison closed the door. Footsteps came up the stairs and along the passage, but not this passage. He heard the man mounting another flight of stairs. He judged from the conversation that there was a guard in the hall; it was probable there would be others at the doors, but it did not sound as if there were one at this landing.

He opened the door again, and a faint light shone against his eyes. He could not pick out shapes, but the glow gave him fresh heart. He turned left, for that was away from the staircase on which he had heard the footsteps so clearly that he guessed his room must be the first one in the passage. And if Anne were still 'in the next room' he would find it along here, on the left. He touched his own door, kept his hand against the wall, and crept along until he reached another door.

He tried the handle; the door was locked.

Standing here, unable to see if anyone approached, would be far more dangerous than opening his own door had been; but he had to try. He took out the nail file again, felt for the lock, and touched something cold and hard—a key! The key was in the lock! He grinned to himself, and turned it, waited, but heard no sound, and went inside.

He closed the door.

He stood quite still, listening for the sound of Anne breathing, and heard it, soft and gentle. He took a step towards the sound. He might stumble into a chair, might kick against the bed, might——

The breathing was interrupted; and Anne stirred.

Rollison said softly, "Anne, don't shout."

A pause, and then, "Who——"

"It's Rollison!"

"Rollison!" she gasped, and the bed creaked.

Now that he was here, he began to wonder whether he was wise to trust her, but there was nothing else he could do.

"How—how did you get here?" Anne demanded huskily.

"Never mind. Anne, do you really want to help?"

"If only I *can*!"

"You can—by being my eyes. I want to see Jolly."

"He's—he's on the next floor up," she said.

"Is there a guard there?"

"I don't think so."

He heard rustling sounds, as if she were donning her dressing-gown. Then she came towards him and took his hand. They walked together to the door, and the light shone against his eyes as they stepped into the passage. He turned and looked at her—and he could see the outline of her head and shoulders. A wild exultation filled him, but he showed no sign.

She held his arm tightly, and whispered: "We'll have to go to the landing, the man in the hall might see us. Keep very quiet. You—you'd better get behind me, and hold my hand."

They went along slowly. He could imagine the scene: the man sitting in the hall, unaware of what was happening. Anne peering towards him. She whispered again, "We're going to turn right, and then go up the stairs." He rubbed against the wall all the time; they reached the corner, turned right, reached the stairs and began to climb them, one at a time. The rustling of her dressing-gown seemed very loud now. Up—up—up. He counted twelve steps, and then she said, "We're at the top." She led him forward again, and whispered: "This is Higginbottom's room. George is next door, then Jolly."

"How is Snub?"

"Not—not too bad. Please don't talk."

They passed George's door, and went on to the next one. There was still a little light, although not so much as there had been on the landing, and he could only just make out Anne's head and shoulders.

"Why, the key's in the door!" she exclaimed, and then whispered, "I mustn't talk!"

"Just turn the key and open the door, and leave the rest to me," said Rollison. "Stand by the door ready to warn us if anyone comes."

She obeyed. Rollison stepped into a dark room, and heard a movement—he thought that Jolly had awakened, or else had not been to sleep. He went a few paces further forward, and then called Jolly's name, softly.

"Mr. *Rollison*!" breathed Jolly, almost at once.

"Yes, it's all safe—but don't put the light on," said Rollison. "Miss Meriton brought me here. Jolly, I want you to get away. There's one guard downstairs in the hall, you can deal with him. I've a message for the police and another for Bill Ebbutt—no one else, do you understand?"

"I—I do indeed, sir."

"Now listen," said Rollison. "For the love of Mike, don't forget the essential points."

"I won't forget," said Jolly softly.

As they stood side by side, each alert for any warning from Anne, Rollison talked swiftly. He outlined Old Harry's story and passed on some of the things he had learned—for instance, that Old Harry did not want to be seen by Anne or anyone else; his war-time background; the fact that he had worn some kind of disguise and was obviously afraid that someone in the house might see through it. And there were other things: that Philip Rowse owned a Lagonda—it was possible that the police already knew that, but he couldn't be sure—that Baxter, Luke and two or three other men were at the house. Jolly interrupted there.

"I know, sir, and I can describe each one I've seen."

"Good—any ideas from you, Jolly?"

"No sir, except——"

"Yes?"

"You ought to come away with me, sir."

"Oh, no," said Rollison. "They still think I'm completely blind; there's a lot more I can do. But you can take George—of course, you *must* take George! And perhaps Anne——"

Jolly said, "Mr. Rollison, did you say——"

"Take George and Anne," said Rollison. "I'll be all right."

"Did you say they *think* you're still blind?" asked Jolly in a hushed voice, and Rollison felt the tightening grip of his fingers.

Rollison smiled in the darkness.

"I'm beginning to see again, and I think I can pull one or two surprises," he said. "Anyhow, Old Harry put that proposition to me, so, for the time being, Luke and the others won't try any rough stuff, even when they've discovered that you've gone. Tell Grice and Ebbutt that I might pretend to help Old Harry—because if he's really organized so thoroughly it's a big business, and even if Old Harry were caught it would still go on. We've got to get them all, and while I'm in their camp I've a chance to do that. It will need plenty of patience, but it can be done."

"Yes, sir," said Jolly, and added uneasily, "but I'm not sure that you can help; you may not be able to see properly for some time, it's too great a risk."

"We're going to take it," said Rollison. "How long will it take you to get dressed?"

"A *very* few minutes," said Jolly. He did not argue any further. "Shall I then warn Armitage——"

"I'll see to him," said Rollison.

Jolly said: "If I may say so, sir, I think you ought to leave that to me. It is just possible that he cannot be relied on, or else that he will be persuaded, later, to tell Old Harry that you helped to free him. It would be much better if he didn't know. We must reduce the risk to the lowest possible degree, sir."

Rollison said: "Yes. All right, Jolly. He's in the room next to you."

"You ought to return to your room, sir, because if the alarm is raised they'll come straight for you."

"I'll get back soon," said Rollison. "Good hunting, Jolly."

Rollison turned and went softly towards the crack of light at the side of the door. He could see that now. He whispered to Anne, who said that she had heard nothing. And he told her that he wanted her to go away with Jolly and George.

Anne said: "No, I shall stay. If I were to go, anything might happen to my uncle. I want to help, but I won't leave. Jolly can do everything necessary outside."

And he knew that there would be no point in arguing with her.

  .   .   .   .   .

Rollison stood in the shadow of a large wardrobe on the landing. He could see a little—the outline of the light, for instance, and the faint glow it made. He could even make out the shape of a picture on the wall, but thought little of that as he waited. He was between the wardrobe and a doorway, hidden from anyone who came down the second flight of stairs, or along either of the passages—he could be seen only by anyone who came out of the nearest room.

Anne was back in her room.

He had wiped the key clean of finger-prints, and locked her in again; it was better that no one should know she had played any part in this escape.

He heard nothing, but suddenly a shadowy figure showed near the light—and then another. Jolly and George—and he could just hear George breathing with suppressed excitement. Jolly whispered something, and George's breathing quietened. The figures moved down the stairs— until Rollison could not see them. The man in the hall hadn't noticed them yet, or he would have raised the alarm.

The silence was brooding, filled with suspense and fears. Rollison took a step forward, would have gone nearer to the stairs, in the hope that he could see what happened, but thought he heard a sound, so drew back again. The silence was even tenser now. He stared at the top of the landing— and then heard a scuffle, a cry which was cut short, a thud— and a chair falling over.

The scuffling sound continued, but there was no further cry until George said in a pent-up whisper: "Got him!"

Jolly didn't speak; nor did George speak again.

Rollison stared at the landing—and then saw what had caused the first noise which had driven him back here. A man was at the head of the stairs. He could see the fellow vaguely, a short, squat shape—probably Luke. He thought that the man's arm was thrust forward, as it might be if he held a gun in his hand.

He left his hiding-place.

He had to move quickly, even if he attracted the fellow's attention.

The outline became clearer. He could see that the squat man had started to walk down the stairs. He could hear sounds from the hall, a key turning, a lock squeaking a little as it was pushed back, the clink of a chain. The man was now a little lower, but Rollison was only just behind him.

Should he trip him up?

If he did, the man would shout and attract the attention of others. And he might get into the grounds soon enough to shoot the two escaping men.

Rollison took a desperate chance.

He judged where the man's neck was, shot out his hands, and gripped. His fingers closed round the flesh of the neck; he heard the man gasp—yes, it was Luke! He got a firm grip with both hands and squeezed; Luke kicked and tried to pull himself free, but the grip was too strong. Rollison braced himself to stand where he was. Luke's struggles grew fiercer, but Rollison's fingers were tight against his windpipe. He could hear the man gasping for breath, trying to draw in the precious air. He thought he heard George exclaim, and Jolly say:

"Never mind that—hurry!"

Luke got home with a stinging blow to the stomach with his elbow. Rollison squeezed—and as he did so he realized that if Luke lived after this he would know who had attacked him—that the prisoner could see. That mustn't happen—here was a man in his grasp, fighting convulsively for breath; a man who must die because of the harm he could do.

A cold wind swept up from the front door.

He could make out Luke's head, even his nose, for Luke was leaning back against him, struggling very little now.

Rollison dragged him back, off the stairs, but still held him in that terrible grip.

Luke stopped struggling.

He went limp.

Rollison let him fall softly to the floor, then bent down and dragged him by the shoulders towards the wardrobe. He let him fall again, then ran his hand over the dark front of the wardrobe until he touched the handle. He pulled it open and felt inside—there were some clothes, but it wasn't full. He lifted Luke inside, then closed and locked the door.

The cold wind no longer blew up the stairs; Jolly and George had closed the front door.

Rollison heard a groan; that would be from the man in the hall. He turned slowly, because he did not feel confident of moving fast, towards the passage and his room.

As he reached the passage he heard a shout, followed by a shot in the grounds.

CHAPTER XVIII

ANGRY OLD HARRY

THE police did not discover the place until the middle of the morning. They found it deserted—or they thought it was, at first. They discovered a huge pile of charred papers in a grate in an upstairs room, and plenty of evidence of hurried departure. They even found a torn envelope addressed to Baxter, but nothing else until Grice arrived in person. Grice ordered that every possible hiding-place should be searched—it was possible that Rollison and the girl had been killed and hidden.

They found Luke, his mouth slack, his eyes half-open and glazed, his neck swollen and purple from the pressure of his killer's fingers, and his body already stiff with *rigor mortis*. They recognized Luke, too—he was an ex-convict, who had served two terms of imprisonment, one for robbery with violence. He had at one time led a small gang, but apparently he had given that up, to work for Old Harry. Every one of Luke's relatives and friends were questioned, but they learned nothing more about his recent activities.

They also found Snub, with a bullet wound in his thigh and another in his shoulder; he had been left for dead, but was alive.

.   .   .   .   .

Jolly had not disturbed Ebbutt during the night, but telephoned him at his little house near the gymnasium in the Mile End Road just after nine o'clock next morning. He warned him that Rollison might pretend to help Old Harry, begged Ebbutt—and it was a considerable effort for Jolly to *beg* the Cockney to do anything—to arrange that everyone whom Rollison approached in the next few days

should do exactly what Rollison requested. Ebbutt
promised that he would, replaced the receiver and, in the
tiny hall of his house let out a string of blasphemous oaths
which called a sharp reproof from his wife, who was washing
up after breakfast. Bill's wife was in the 'Army', and there
was no salvation for men who persisted in taking God's
name in vain.

.   .   .   .   .

Rollison could see a little better even than he had on the
journey through the night to London. Then he had picked
out the shapes of the telegraph poles and the dark shapes
beyond the beams of the headlights. He had known that
after a while they were travelling along a main road through
a built-up area. He saw the difference between shopping
centres and residential districts, and once he saw the huge
outline of a building which he took to be a cinema. These
buildings had become more frequent after a while.

He had known that he was in London. . . .

He was still in London, and somewhere near the Strand.

He had been brought here, to a narrow alley, and ushered
into an even narrower passage, then taken down a flight of
stairs, along other passages into this room. He could not
see much here, because there was little light—only one dim
lamp was lit. He thought it was a lounge or drawing-room,
although once he had knocked himself against a sharp edge
which felt like the corner of a desk.

Anne was no longer with him.

He had been here for some time, dozing occasionally,
never brooding on what was likely to happen when he next
saw Old Harry. There was not the slightest reason for suspecting that Old Harry would think he had played any
part in the escape—but he knew Jolly had been successful,
or he would not have been brought away from the country
house.

He wished he knew what had happened to Anne.

He stifled a yawn, eased his position—and then heard

footsteps echoing along a wooden-floored passage. He sat upright, waiting, heard the door open and Old Harry say: "Put on the light."

That split second of warning saved Rollison from giving himself away. He closed his eyes, so that when the light flashed on he did not blink.

He looked at Old Harry through his lashes.

He saw a man of medium height, with long, black hair and a black beard; obviously both were false. He was broader than Rollison had pictured; by no means a small man. His features seemed to be large, but Rollison could not be sure. They were very vague and became vaguer the more he looked. He turned his gaze away as Old Harry had approached.

The man who had come with him went out, shutting the door.

Rollison did not look round the room nor straight at Old Harry. But he saw that it was a small room with no windows—partly office, partly sitting-room. Old Harry came and stood very close to him—too close for comfort.

"You think yourself *very* clever, Rollison," he said.

"I think I'm very dull," said Rollison tartly. "I suppose you had a scare, or you wouldn't have moved me in such a hurry."

"So you don't know what happened," said Old Harry softly.

"I know that I was dragged out of bed in the middle of the night, pushed into some clothes and bustled out of the house," said Rollison testily. "If I could only see, I'd make you and your roughnecks treat me more gently."

"But you can't see," said Old Harry. "You mustn't let yourself forget that for a moment, Rollison. But I don't believe you know nothing about it. Your man Jolly escaped and took Armitage with him, and—and he killed Luke. The body was found. My best man, Rollison— Jolly killed him."

Rollison cried, "*What?*"

"And before I'm through I will make Jolly suffer as you've never conceived suffering," said Old Harry. "I do not threaten for the sake of it—I do not like cruelty for its own sake, as Luke did; but to kill him—you'll understand what I mean when you hear Jolly scream, when you hear him crying out for mercy!"

"If you hurt Jolly, you won't get any help from me," said Rollison harshly.

Old Harry did not speak for what seemed a long time. When he did, his voice had lost the harsh and angry note, and was soft and gentle again.

"So you've decided, have you?" he asked. "You value your sight more than your ideals—oh, these oft-vaunted ideals! They soon vanish when a man's life is at stake." He laughed a little, as if from reaction.

"I'll hear your proposition," said Rollison.

"You won't hear it yet," said Old Harry. "Rollison, I don't think you understand quite what last night's incidents amount to. I've lost Luke, my best contact man with the fools in the East End. Apart from that, *you've* been busy among the East Enders."

"Don't be a fool," said Rollison roughly. "I've been helpless here."

"Your past intruded," said Old Harry. "The East Enders think you are going to their help again, Rollison. I've had them scared, through Luke and others. I've had them so worried that a lot of them have done what I wanted them to do, but now—they think Rollison's behind them; they've a silly, touching faith in Rollison. I want control of the East End and I can't get it because of *you*."

Rollison said, "Then Jolly——"

"I don't care whether Jolly did it, or whether you did it before I caught you," said Old Harry, "but it's happened. You're the knight errant of the slums, Rollison—and at a word from you they'll do what I tell them. I didn't realize before how strong your hold was, but I realize it now."

"Well?" said Rollison.

"I'll tell you what I want you to do a little later," said Old Harry. "Just remember this, Rollison. If you fail me, you won't ever see again. If you fail me, I shall catch Jolly and teach him the consequences of killing Luke, and——"

A new sound came into the room; a cry from a woman. It was high-pitched, frightened; and it stopped abruptly. Rollison turned towards the door; Old Harry stopped speaking.

"No, no!" It was Anne, and she sounded terrified.

"You'll stop them hurting that girl," Rollison growled. "There are limits to what I'll stand."

"There aren't any limits to what you'll have to stand," said Old Harry. "You're quite helpless, Rollison, keep remembering that."

"No!" screamed Anne, and she sounded right outside the door now. "I can't stand it, I can't stand it!"

Rollison stood up slowly, his hands clenched. A vein stood out in his forehead and pulsed madly. His breathing was laboured. He could have flung himself forward at Old Harry and treated him just as he had treated Luke, but—something stopped him. He hardly knew what it was, but stopped himself from acting then. Anne's cries grew fainter, she was being taken away.

Then Rollison saw something glint in the light; he had hardly seen anything like that since his blindness. It was a flash, which came across his eyes.

It was a knife.

Old Harry was going to use it, he——

No, he was putting it away.

Old Harry said gently: "Think well, Rollison. You—Jolly—and the girl will all suffer if you fail me. Fond of that girl, aren't you? You always had a reputation for liking the ladies, and if you could see her you'd realize how lovely she is. But—she'll suffer like you're suffering unless you do what you're told. All three of you. And this time you won't be able to escape, I've taken good care of that. I'm taking personal charge now, to make sure that nothing else goes wrong. Understand me, Rollison?"

Rollison said thickly, "Yes."

"You'd better," said Old Harry. "To make big business of crime, there's one big thing I need. Most Cockneys are honest"—he sneered the word—"but few will give away a criminal to the police. They've got to be on my side, Rollison. They've been on yours, these innocents; now I'm going to win their trust with your help."

He laughed, turned away, went softly to the door, and let himself out.

The key turned in the lock.

He had left the light *on*.

But Rollison did not pay any attention to the room then. He sat down heavily, and mopped the sweat from his forehead. That had been a deliberate test—Anne had been threatened or hurt, he did not believe she had been pretending. Old Harry had wondered if he were bluffing, whether he could see, and had believed he would act if he heard those screams. That sixth sense which had kept him standing still had saved him from the knife.

Old Harry's assessment of East Enders was shrewd. Rollison knew that all he had said was true. Once the whole district was solidly behind the man, he was absolutely safe from disclosure.

Now—some of the crooks were taking Old Harry's orders; he had known that, he must find out which ones they were. He must find out where the solicitors, the shipping agents, the jewellers and the others who were within the organization, could be found. When this job was finished, it must be a clean sweep; even catching Old Harry wasn't enough.

He did not think he would have been able to catch Old Harry then. He remembered the glint of the knife, which he hadn't noticed because of his poor vision—he was still at the man's mercy, even though he could see a little.

He looked round the room now.

There were three hide armchairs, in one of which he was sitting, a radio, a cocktail cabinet, a small revolving book-case. The desk was clear of papers; two empty letter-trays stood on it, with a large blotting-pad; that was all. There was no telephone in the room. Some cheap coloured prints hung on the cream-washed walls, and behind the desk was a large picture calendar.

There were no windows.

And he had to wait again.

CHAPTER XIX

GATHERING OF CROOKS

Probably no man knew more about the rumours and the anxieties rife in the East End of London than Bill Ebbutt. He heard most rumours very quickly—he had been one of the first to hear about the influence of Old Harry, and to tell Rollison about that mysterious gentleman of whom so many had heard but whom no one appeared to have seen.

Bill had been busy that day, spreading the news among the trusty that Rollison might appear to do something that was out of character. And he had also been busy listening to rumours—and one reached him in the middle of the afternoon. It came from Wally the Dog—a nickname given to Wally because, when angry, he would growl remarkably like a savage brute ready to spring.

Although Wally's bark was much worse than his bite, there was one other thing about him which made many people nervous of his nearness. He was remarkable as a 'dip'. That is, he could pick pockets with a sleight-of-hand which made even practised dip-men gasp. Many a wallet had been stolen by Wally without there being the slightest suspicion in the mind of his victim that he was being robbed.

But Wally was getting old.

What was more, he had nearly been caught twice in the past six months. Because he was more sinned against than sinning, for he had been sent to a reform school at the tender age of nine and had learned most of his tricks there, Bill Ebbutt helped him to run straight.

Wally had shown every sign of doing this—and yet he had received an order, a few days before, from Old Harry. He had told Ebbutt about this, and Ebbutt had told him to report when his next order came through. The first was simply that he should be ready to do a job whenever Old Harry sent word.

About half past four, Wally the Dog slunk into the gymnasium, a huge wood-and-corrugated-iron building which was, surprisingly, almost empty at the time. The door of the small office, in a corner, was ajar, and Bill Ebbutt was talking to three cronies when Wally appeared in the doorway. He was small, thin, dejected-looking, and a blackened, hand-made cigarette drooped from his thin lips. His words were ejected from them in a low-pitched growl.

"Spare me a minnit, Bill?"

"Sure," said Ebbutt, looking up.

"Want ter see yer alone."

"Oke," said Ebbutt. "Okay, boys."

His cronies, three in number, passed Wally, who shut the door.

"Well, wot's on yer mind?" asked Ebbutt.

"Thought yer oughta know," growled Wally. "Got me ordis. Got to go to Swann's ware'ouse ter-night."

" 'E can't expect yer to pick up much there," said Ebbutt, who was massive behind a small, cheap, deal desk which was wildly untidy.

"Ain't the only one going," said Wally. "Met free-four more. All meeting at Swann's. Watcher fink I better do?"

The implication was clear enough: Wally and others were to gather at Swann's warehouse, and gathering was not a habit favoured by crooks. Yet they would obey Old Harry. The obvious thing to do was to warn the police that a visit to the warehouse should bring in good results, but Wally knew quite well that he need fear nothing like that from Ebbutt. The trainer would not lift a finger to let the police round up a number of men at a time, unless he were convinced they were all bad beyond the pale. Bill Ebbutt's idea of 'bad' did not coincide with the conception held by the police or the average citizen.

"Fought yer might tell the Torf, if 'e's free," growled Wally.

"Maybe I will," said Ebbutt. "Wally, you go along, and tell me what 'appens, will yer? Just that—if Old Harry gives yer a job, yer'd better take it, but let me know."

"Okay," said Wally.

.   .   .   .   .

Swann's warehouse was now derelict. It was near the docks, and could be approached from three different directions, all of which could be guarded by scouts. It was used for gaming; for handing over hot loot; for passing on messages. Yet it had been used so carefully that the police did not know this.

Now a constant stream of men went to one or the other of the three entrances, walked across the creaky, rotting floor to a door, and down a flight of cement steps to the cellar. This was one huge room, which had been white-washed many, many years before. Huge cobwebs hung in the corners and from the rafters. There was a musty smell, and the huge cellar struck cold, in spite of the fact that when Wally the Dog slipped in, at least twenty others were there.

It was an astonishing gathering of rogues. Some, like Wally, looked as if they hadn't two pennies to rub together, and that their mouths were dry for the price of a drink. They wore old cloth caps and chokers, and their clothes were ragged. There were others who looked spruce and clean. These wore suits of Italian cut, with exotic ties, and had, almost without exception, elaborately styled hair.

There was, in addition, a sprinkling of well-dressed men who looked out of place in this company; these were the confidence tricksters who worked the West End, and whose accent could compete with anything created by Oxford and—in the opinion of their owners—often improved upon that.

They were of all sizes and shapes. One little man, dressed

like Wally, was no more than four feet six inches tall, and could easily have been taken for a boy. He was a clever and most daring cat-burglar.

Wally went up to him, and was so affected that he did not growl.

"Cor!" said the cat-burglar.

"Strike a ruddy light!" gasped Wally.

More men slipped in; footsteps clattered down the stairs. There was obvious uneasiness; none here failed to realize the disaster that would follow a police-raid. Most of them had known that several others would be present; none had dreamed that it would be a gathering like this. Men who had picked oakum in every jail of England, Scotland and Wales were gathered together. There was Labouche, the little French jewel-thief, who had lived in London for twenty years and still hardly knew a word of English—or professed that he didn't—and whose sly, sideways glance was known and disliked throughout the East End.

There was a babble of low-pitched talk; too much noise would attract attention outside while the doors upstairs were open.

No one had entered for ten minutes, and the hands of thirty or forty watches pointed to seven-thirty. Those who hadn't watches glanced at their neighbour's.

Then there was a stir from the far end of the cellar, where there was a blocked entrance. In front of this was a raised platform, once used for a weighing machine; it was large enough to hold a dozen men.

A door, which hadn't been known to open for years, creaked and swung inwards—and Baxter appeared. Behind him came a man with a huge, black beard and flowing, black hair and behind him——

A hiss of surprise went up from the crowd.

There was not a man here who did not know Rollison by sight. Most of them knew him well; at least half of them hated him. Several were the original owners of trophies which now adorned the wall at Gresham Terrace. But, whether they hated him, or whether they liked him for some service he had rendered to them, a friend or a relative, there was not a man present who did not own an admiration for the Toff. Reluctant it might be; but they knew him as a man of unswerving purpose and great courage, of endless resource and a curious ability to work on their nerves to frighten and alarm. His visiting-card was as familiar as a policeman's helmet.

He walked slowly forward, without aid, and looked round at them. He smiled slightly, nodded here and there, but did not look any man straight in the face.

"Hallo, boys," he said.

Yes, it was Rollison; his face, his voice, his immaculate clothes, even his smile; but there was something about him which none of those present had ever seen before, and they could not place it.

No one answered him.

"Now just a moment, Rolly," said Old Harry in his soft, gentle voice. It carried surprisingly well, and reached the ears of the men who stood near the entrance, ready to make a rush for it if there was an alarm. "First I want a word with you all," continued Old Harry. "You needn't be scared of a raid, I've got runners out all over the place; if more than a couple of dicks get together within half a mile of this room I shall know about it. All clear, boys?"

No one responded.

Wally's mouth was open and his tongue showed; he lived up to his name more than ever.

"Good, good," said Old Harry. "Now, Mr. Rollison wants to say a few words—you all know him, don't you? He's a very good sort—better than some of you realized, I expect." Old Harry gave a curious little chuckle. "Now, Rolly," he said.

Rollison stepped forward.

There was a stir among the crowd. Everyone stared at his solitary figure, and none realized that he could see only a

blur of faces and bodies, and couldn't pick out any in-
dividual. He smiled again. . . .

.   .   .   .   .

Rollison smiled with an effort, because he didn't like this
situation at all. He could see so little, but he knew that
there were between forty and fifty men in the room, because Baxter had reported that only a few minutes before
they had made their entry. Baxter had named a few of
them too, including Labouche, Wally the Dog, Karn, the
cat-burglar—and others whose names were written as large
on the Toff's mind as they were on the records at Scotland
Yard. He knew that some would gladly have cut his throat,
that others would have gone to jail rather than hurt or
betray him.

And now he had to persuade them to work for Old
Harry.

He said, "We needn't spend a lot of time, boys; you
aren't happy about staying together too long, in spite of
what Old Harry says."

A silence—a sigh—and then on a dozen lips the echo:
"Old Harry." Heads turned towards the man with the
black beard.

Old Harry beamed at them, and showed very white
teeth—they looked too white to be natural.

"All I've got to say is this," said Rollison. "You all
work on your own, or in twos and threes. You're at the
mercy of fences who cut you down and give you a quarter,
often less, of what your stuff is worth. You have to take it
because you can't find another market and the fences are all
the same, they buy low. That's right, isn't it?"

He had succeeded in doing what had appeared impossible
a moment before—he had taken their attention from Old
Harry.

He had touched on the one grievance about which they all
agreed—the iniquity of fences, the difficulty of selling their
'goods' at reasonable prices while they were hot.

So they listened to him.

"Of course it's right," said Rollison. "And there's more to it than that, you know. Working on your own, you're likely to get caught—by the police or by me." He gave a laugh which sounded natural enough to everyone present, although it came strangely from his lips. "I've changed sides," he went on. "I tried to help a lot of you against the police, but they never give you a square deal."

He paused, rather like a music-hall artist waiting for applause or laughter—and he won a growl of agreement. Victimization by the police was a fallacy deeply imprinted on their minds.

"You all know me," went on Rollison. "There are some crimes I won't tolerate, but others—well, it's your job, and you've had a raw deal, that's why you do it. All right, then —make a good thing of it. You don't like being ordered about, and I think Old Harry made a mistake when he blackmailed some of you into working for him, but—he's always given you your fair share of the proceeds, hasn't he?" No one spoke, no one responded in any way. "Come on, let's hear from anyone who hasn't received what Old Harry promised him for a job."

There was no response.

Rollison raised his hands.

"There you are, then," he said cheerfully. "And you'll find it safe working with Old Harry. He's got lawyers to defend you if you get caught; he'll look after your wives and the kids; he'll see you through, and he'll lay you off when things get hot. You won't have to worry about selling your goods; all you'll have to do is the job he puts up—and if you tell him it's not the right job for you he'll give you another one. Won't you, Harry?"

"Yes," said Old Harry, "I will gladly do that. I want everyone to be happy."

Rollison said: "You'll be a gang of fools if you don't work with Old Harry. He and Baxter have something to say to you now . . ." He paused when Old Harry whispered to him, and then grinned broadly, and said: "All right, I'll say it. There's a job for each one of you, *tonight*. Baxter will tell you the place and tell you what you're after—and where to take the stuff when you've finished. All right, then—good hunting!"

And he turned away.

Only one or two noticed that a man in the doorway helped him out of the cellar.

.   .   .   .   .

It was not until the next morning that Jolly learned of the meeting. Bill Ebbutt told him in person, while George Armitage, who was staying at the flat, waited in another room. Outside, the antiquated Ford stood like a relic of a bygone age, and in the study, beneath the trophy wall, Ebbutt talked earnestly.

If his news shocked Jolly he saw no evidence of it, and Jolly lost no time in saying that obviously Mr. Rollison had something like this in mind when he had sent the message. But when Bill had gone, walking laboriously downstairs and cranking up the engine before it would start, Jolly stayed for some time in the study. He did not feel like talking to Armitage yet. He could not understand what had happened, unless Rollison had been frightened into talking to that crowd of criminals; and, to Jolly, the thought that his beloved Rollison could be frightened into doing anything, even to save his sight, was unthinkable.

It was clearly impossible to say anything of this to the police. Even Grice, friendly though he was, would not be able to acquiesce in such a move.

During the day many reports came in of burglaries and hold-ups, smash-and-grabs—some big, some small. The evening newspapers were filled with the stories which appeared like a rash on front and inside pages.

Naturally, George Armitage noticed it.

He was a trying companion at the flat, not because he was cowardly now, but because he was restless, anxious to be up

and doing. He embarrassed Jolly, as he had once embarrassed Snub, by flaying himself with remorse. This was
all his fault. Rollison, Snub and Anne in danger because
he had been a craven fool.

Anne.

Jolly knew that George Armitage was thinking a great
deal about the girl.

CHAPTER XX

THE POLICE GET THEIR MAN

THE wave of crime on the one night, coming so swiftly upon Rollison's warning, shook Grice and the Yard and the police in the Divisions. But something else shook them much more; there was no clue of any kind to the identity of the thieves—except the general indications that this job or that was the work of a certain known man. For instance, they knew that Labouche had broken into a house in Portman Square and taken three thousand five hundred pounds' worth of jewellery while the owner slept, because the Frenchman had a particular way of blocking all doors open to ensure a swift escape if an alarm were raised. That was Labouche's trade-mark, but it wasn't evidence which would even get him committed for trial, and they could find nothing else.

The thieves had been extremely careful, and Grice, sitting in his office overlooking the Embankment, on the second morning after the crimes, told the Assistant Commissioner that he had never known anything organized on such a scale. If this were a sample of how Old Harry planned to work the police were going to have a bad time.

"Of course, Grice," said the A.C., an affable man with a stubborn mind. "Of course you're worried, but I shouldn't take this too seriously if I were you. You've rather a tendency to be overawed by Rollison's suggestions, you know."

Grice could have replied rudely; instead he argued.

"I've always had reason to take him seriously," he said. "And we shouldn't forget that he's stayed in Old Harry's hands so as to try to make a clean sweep of the job, when he could have come away and left us to clear up the mess."

"Ah, yes—*could* have. Not like Rollison to take that way out, though." The A.C. twirled his long brown moustache. "There would be no kudos that way. Brilliant man, of course, but—well, he should have left all this to us. *All* this. Asked for trouble, so he can't complain if he gets it."

Grice was stung.

"I've never known Rollison take first knock when it would really have helped if he'd put us in, sir. I've often felt angry with him, but he's always justified himself."

The A.C. looked through his ginger lashes.

"All right, Grice, we mustn't argue about it."

Grice was saved the need for comment by the ringing of the telephone. He took the receiver off quickly.

"Hallo, Grice. Patton here—we've picked up Labouche. And would you believe it, he had some stuff on him!" The chief inspector at the other end of the wire was excusably excited. "Want to see him?"

"*Do* I!" exclaimed Grice.

"I'll bring him over in twenty minutes," promised Chief Inspector Patton.

.   .   .   .   .

Labouche was frightened; Labouche talked—of a gathering of crooks, and of Rollison.

.   .   .   .   .

The Assistant Commissioner was not just stubborn now, and he certainly wasn't affable. He was angry, and showed it. Not with Grice—he took a pitying view of Grice's trust in Rollison—but with Rollison. Whatever his motives, to persuade a gang of criminals to give allegiance to Old Harry was unforgivable. In any case, where was the justification for assuming that his motives were good? Rollison could have escaped from the country house, but preferred not to; he had delayed informing the police until the last minute, leaving it too late for them to do very much. And now—he had actually connived at this outbreak. First warned the police it was coming, then arranged it! There ought to be a warrant out for him.

Grice, who knew when it was safe to argue, sat tight-lipped under the tirade, and did not even point out that they couldn't issue a warrant on a statement from Labouche. But he knew that the A.C. was furious—and not long after he had left his office he heard from a sergeant that the story of Rollison talking to the gathering of crooks was already going the rounds.

Worse followed.

The East End 'closed up' completely.

Until then there had been some rumours about Old Harry because there were grievances against him, but now all that was over. The East End could be the most stubborn and sullen area in the world. It could cover itself with a curtain of silence about any one thing, and the police from the Yard or from the Division couldn't pierce it. For the first time for months there was no murmur of bitterness against Old Harry.

There was no word from Rollison.

Jolly and Armitage were closely watched, but Rollison did not get in touch with them.

Grice himself visited Philip Rowse's flat, but could not force Rowse into admitting anything, although there was evidence that his Lagonda had been out on the night of the Brayling crime.

From Rowse, after a long and stormy interview, Grice went to see Anne Meriton's uncle. Rowse had named Anne; so had Snub, who was still seriously ill, but off the danger-list—like Clara. So Grice decided to see the old man.

. . . . . .

Richard Grey was in fact a young-old man; he had a bushy white beard and a shining, nearly-bald head, bright blue eyes—which showed his anxiety, in spite of their brightness. He sat in a book-lined room in his house at Muswell Hill, and talked. . . .

"Yes, Superintendent, I'm glad you've come; I ought to have told you about Anne days ago, and yet—I hoped for the best, you know. They haven't actually hurt her, and she is allowed to telephone me each day. She pretends to be reassuring, but I know how frightened she must be. Yes." He drew at his curved pipe. "And now that I know Anne is in danger, then I must forget my own worries and anxieties and make a full confession—I think that's the word."

"Confession?" echoed Grice.

Grey smiled a little wanly.

"Yes, Superintendent. You see—I know Old Harry."

Grice jumped up.

"Are you serious?"

"Oh, yes, yes—most serious. But I can't tell you his other name, or where he lives, or even what he looks like, he is always disguised—rather clumsily, but at least it makes sure that no one knows what he really looks like. He's been blackmailing me for years. An old indiscretion. I will make a statement about that later, if you like."

"The reason doesn't matter much—the fact that Old Harry has been after you does," said Grice, towering over him.

"Let me tell you the story in my own words," pleaded Grey, and proceeded to tell Grice what Anne had told Rollison, except that he did not name Rowse as the go-between who collected the money from him. He told how Anne had tried to help, how she had unknowingly allowed herself to be drawn into Old Harry's clutches, and:

"She's a very lovely girl, and loves life—naturally. I haven't been able to give her everything I should like to give her; I've just been able to keep going comfortably here," went on Grey. "This blackmail has been a constant drain on me, Superintendent, a *constant* drain. Once I was wealthy—now!" He threw up his hands. "I was a fool ever to tell her the truth, I should have deceived her. Now, trying to help me, she has got herself into grave danger, and I shall never forgive myself."

"You can forgive yourself if you'll help us to find her," Grice said. "Have you had a visit from Old Harry or his agent since she disappeared?"

"No."

"All right," said Grice. "You say that Old Harry has called once or twice in person, but usually uses this agent— the same man. Who is this agent?"

Richard Grey sat down heavily.

"Very well," he said in an unsteady voice. "It is Philip Rowse."

Grice snapped: "Is Rowse Old Harry?"

Grey started. "*Rowse?* Why, it didn't occur to me, but— it *could* be. He's about the same build, and—but I really don't know, Superintendent, I'm only guessing."

"All right," said Grice. "What do you know of Webb— *Harry* Webb? He came to see you over this blackmail, didn't he?"

The young-old man nodded.

"Yes, he was the instigator of it. He was always a man of dubious habits—he had been soured by some war-time experience, I believe—or, rather, post-war experience."

Grice let him talk, although there was nothing new said about Harry Webb. The commission agent hadn't returned to his office, and a nation-wide call was out for him. The possibility that he was Old Harry couldn't be ignored, but now Rowse had to be considered.

He left Grey a sad, sorrowful-looking man.

.   .   .   .   .

Grice did not go immediately to Rowse's Garron Street flat, but went to the Yard to check up on what had already been discovered about the owner of the Lagonda. He reflected, as he sat at his desk, that the murder of the servant girl had assumed a far greater importance than had ever seemed likely and yet, in one way, had dropped out of the limelight. It was the same with the girl reporter, Clara Mickle. She was recovering slowly, and certainly wouldn't die—but as far as this case was concerned she no longer mattered.

Philip Rowse. . . .

A man with innumerable *affaires*, which were a byword; nothing was known against him. He did not work, but was director of a number of small companies—including an export company, and several distributing firms which might be useful for the disposal of stolen goods. He was also a director of a Birmingham and a Glasgow firm of jewellers, of two dress shops—in fact his finger appeared to be in every sort of pie. There were several small strings of provincial hotels which had the name of Philip Rowse on their list of directors.

Grice felt a growing excitement.

Rollison had told him, through Jolly, how carefully Old Harry had prepared to market the stolen goods, and Rowse was certainly in a position to help a great deal. Rowse might have fooled Rollison and Anne—might be a prominent agent of Old Harry, even Old Harry himself.

He went along to Garron Street, where Rowse's flat was being watched. At the corner a sergeant beckoned him, and Grice approached.

"Is he in?" he asked.

"He's in all right," said the sergeant. "A woman's just gone in too, sir. Ripe piece!"

"Not Miss Meriton?" Hope flared.

"Oh, no, sir. Should have said over-ripe! Just the kind he fancies, according to what I've heard."

"I'll go and see what they're talking about," said Grice.

"Talking!" grinned the sergeant.

Outside the flat, Grice kept his finger on the bell. Foster, Rowse's poker-faced manservant, opened the door.

"Mr. Rowse," said Grice.

"I'm sorry, sir, Mr. Rowse is not——"

Grice pushed past him.

"Now don't ask for trouble," he said, and for a moment the servant's face lost its composure. Grice strode across the hall towards the drawing-room. He flung the door open, fully aware that he himself was asking for trouble by forcing his way into the flat, and that Rowse might be able to make things difficult for him. Yet Rowse stood near the fireplace, gaping; the 'ripe piece' stared at Grice with horrified alarm.

On a table between them was a small heap of precious stones, sparkling and scintillating.

.   .   .   .   .

They were all stolen jewels.

Rowse was charged with receiving, the 'ripe piece' for being in possession of stolen goods knowing them to have been stolen. And a check up was made on all Rowse's *inamoratas*. They were, it appeared, messengers who brought jewels from Old Harry to Rowse, who valued them.

One or two of them knew Old Harry as a man with a bushy black beard.

None could swear that Rowse, disguised, wasn't Old Harry. None knew much—if anything—about Webb. Webb had always remained a figure in the background—a name rather than a person. Yet he had been seen, daily, by his staff. The available description might have fitted Old Harry, without the black beard. He might even be Rowse, cleverly disguised, but Grice wasn't at all convinced about that.

Grice couldn't persuade Rowse to talk, and none of the women had visited Rowse anywhere but at Garron Street.

Grice told all this to the Assistant Commissioner, who made one pithy remark.

"It wouldn't surprise me if *Rollison* isn't Old Harry."

"But Rollison and Old Harry were in that cellar at the same time——" began Grice.

"Nonsense," said the A.C. "Any man with a black beard and dark hair could *look* like Old Harry; different men might take on the disguise at different times. Can't you get any line on where Rollison is?"

.   .   .   .   .

Bill Ebbutt lumbered up the stairs at Gresham Terrace and was received by Jolly almost as eagerly as the latter would have received Rollison. He shook his head in answer to Jolly's questioning look, and Jolly stepped aside to let him in. George was visiting Snub at the nursing home.

"No news at all?" asked Jolly.

"Nope," said Bill. "Not wot yer'd call news, Mr. Jolly. Plenty of *rumours.*" He gave the other an odd look.

"There are always rumours," said Jolly.

"There ain't often rumours like this," said Ebbutt, and heaved a gargantuan sigh. "I just can't make it aht, Mr. Jolly. I—look 'ere, you an' me are pals, ain't we?"

Jolly drew back a pace.

"We have always been on very good terms, Mr. Ebbutt, yes."

Ebbutt leaned forward and breathed into his face.

"Mr. Jolly, be honest wiv me. Mr. Ar ain't 'ad a bad time lately, 'as 'e? Lost a packet o' money, or anyfink like that?"

"Not to my knowledge," said Jolly, showing astonished surprise. "What makes you think——"

"I just dunno wot ter think," repeated Ebbutt, "but these 'ere rumours is gettin' very strong, Mr. Jolly. Yer can't turn rahnd wivvout 'earing them. They all say the same thing in diff'rent ways, that Mr. Ar's Old Harry, and the other man's just a stooge. Mr. Ar 'as be'aved pecoolier in this business, ain't 'e?"

CHAPTER XXI

THE TOFF—OR OLD HARRY?

ROLLISON had spent a week in this same room, going out only three times, and then after dark and in a closed car with the blinds drawn, and speaking to meetings of criminals. And after each meeting there had been an outbreak of crimes of all kinds and variety—and he knew from a newspaper left behind by Old Harry that the police had made only one arrest—that of Labouche.

The door of his room was closely guarded.

Anne had not been allowed to come and see him.

And the only way out was through the door.

He looked at himself in the mirror, for the light was on.

He could see himself clearly. The gradual recovery had crept upon him; now he had almost forgotten the horrors of blindness, was concerned only with the way he could turn it to advantage.

He dressed each morning with the light out, so that the careless touches would convince Old Harry that he still could not see. His hair parting was uneven, his collar and tie were awry, the buttons of his waistcoat were in the wrong buttonholes—little touches which were vital.

Each day a little man came in and shaved him, but did not have much to say.

This morning, as he departed, he left behind a copy of the *Morning Echo*, and as soon as the door was locked Rollison picked it up eagerly—but there was no eagerness in his expression when he read the headlines, only a complete dismay.

For the headline read:

THE TOFF—OR OLD HARRY?

Rollison read on with great difficulty, feeling a clammy sweat on his forehead and neck.

It is now ten days since the Hon. Richard Rollison disappeared from his London flat. A week since the first series of organized robberies alarmed Scotland Yard. The police have reason to believe that the organizer is a criminal known as Old Harry—but have they any reason to believe the rumour, prevalent in the East End, that Old Harry is an alias for the Toff—which is an alias of Richard Rollison's?

This rumour is now so strong that the *Morning Echo* believes that its duty is to make it public, because . . .

Rollison finished reading and dropped the paper.

He could easily understand how such a rumour had started; but it must be of great strength now, or the *Morning Echo* would not have taken such risks; this was libel in its most blatant form.

Never mind libel. Did the police really consider——?

He heard footsteps in the passage outside, and thought he heard a gentle voice. For a moment he stared at the door, hating Old Harry—and then his mind began to work quickly. It was unusual for Old Harry to come so early in the morning. He had thought it just carelessness that the paper was left each day, but—was it careless or deliberate? Were they still testing his blindness?

He picked the paper up.

The barber had left it on a corner of the dressing-table, folded with the sporting page on the outside.

He folded it and replaced it.

The door opened. . . .

"Good morning, Mr. Rollison," said Old Harry cheerfully. "And how are you this morning?"

Rollison said abruptly, "I'm getting more than a little tired of being here."

"Yes, yes, I suppose you are, but it really needn't be

much longer now," said Old Harry. He looked into Rollison's eyes, but Rollison stared over his shoulder blankly. He picked up the newspaper, watching Rollison very closely, and Rollison ignored him.

Old Harry chuckled.

"It will be a real pleasure for you to read the newspapers again, won't it, Mr. Rollison?"

"Are they ever worth reading?" asked Rollison.

"Sometimes—oh, yes, sometimes," murmured Old Harry. He put the paper down. "Rollison, I admire you very much indeed. For your calm during these trying days. For your wise acceptance of the inevitable. And perhaps most of all for your influence in the East End. From the time you first appeared on that platform with me there has been a great change. I have met no serious opposition since then, and the third night's sorties have been as successful as the first two. And there will be no serious trouble in future. Now that they are used to taking and obeying orders, they will continue to do so, whether you issue them or I do."

"I'm issuing no more orders," said Rollison.

"Oh no." Old Harry gave a gentle little chuckle. "No, you're issuing no more orders, Rollison. In fact, I don't think I need your help any more."

Rollison said slowly, "You haven't forgotten our bargain, have you?"

"That your sight should be returned," said Old Harry. "No, no, I haven't forgotten. It will come back slowly, in any case, unless you are injected with the serum to make it worse, but I can hasten its recovery. I will do so, tonight I think. Yes, tonight."

Rollison said, "And Anne Meriton?"

"Ah, yes, poor Anne. Always so thoughtful for others, aren't you? But I'm afraid that Anne will have to stay with me. You see, Rollison, she has seen me as I really am. Isn't it remarkable? She started out, a young, innocent, not very intelligent girl, to find me. She was so loyal to her uncle, she took great risks, and succeeded where you failed —she actually set eyes on me! But never mind, she hasn't been ill-treated. If she has to die, she will go peacefully, I do not like cruelty. But let's talk business! I'm calling another meeting tonight, Rollison."

Rollison did not speak.

"Not quite the same kind of meeting," said Old Harry, "but one that's necessary, because I am going away for a little while. I'm going to meet all those who help in the organization. They won't recognize me—I shall remain disguised—but I must tell them exactly what is to be done while I'm away. So far we have dealt with the operatives, now we shall talk to the executives. You'd like to meet them, wouldn't you?"

Rollison said, "I don't care whether I meet them or not."

"Oh, but you must," said Old Harry. "And you must admit how clever I've been. Getting such men as these to work together." He laughed again. "I've always worked in the same way—the way that you call blackmail. A man made a slip; I fastened on to it and pressed him into service. These men who serve are all afraid to disobey, but in any case, few, if any of them, want to now. It is so much more profitable working for me. And tonight, Rollison, you shall see them all."

"You'll use that warehouse once too often," said Rollison.

"Oh, we're not going there again—they're coming here," said Old Harry. "You are at the headquarters now. Everything is directed from here. These living quarters are in the basement, but the business offices are upstairs."

He laughed again.

·   ·   ·   ·   ·

Old Harry had been gone for an hour: Rollison knew that because he could see the hands of the small clock on the desk. The quiet of this room, one of the worst features of the waiting, was getting on his nerves. He was jumpy, because he knew that the time to act was very near.

Old Harry had told the truth about the other meetings: they had taken place. So would this one, and—the police must raid the premises. There would never be another opportunity like it to make a complete round-up.

But—how to get word out?

He went to the door, and knelt down on one knee to examine the lock. It wouldn't be particularly difficult to pick, he would be able to open it with his nail file. But if a man was still on guard he would have no chance. He might deal with the guard, but if he did that he would still have to get clear of the place. The guard would be found, the meeting cancelled.

He tapped on the door.

There was no response.

He tapped again, more loudly, and there was still no answer.

He took out the nail file and began to work on the lock. Now that he could see, he was able to work much more quickly. Soon the lock clicked back. He did not open the door immediately, but tapped again.

Silence.

He opened the door an inch and peered into a narrow passage. A dim light burned at the far end of it. There were two doors, one on either side of the passage, a large radiator, and several pictures on the walls.

He opened the door more widely and stepped into the passage.

It would be so easy to force his way out and not come back, but to get that message away and return to his room as if nothing had happened might prove impossible; it was just something he had to try. He reached the nearer door and tried the handle. The door was locked, but the lock would give no more trouble than that of his own room. He didn't work on it at once, but turned to the opposite door.

This wasn't locked.

He opened it a fraction of an inch, hearing nothing. Another inch, so that he could look inside. He switched on the light. This was a sumptuously furnished bedroom, and no one was here. He slipped inside and closed the door. On the bedside table were two telephones. Telephones—contact with the outside world. His heart beat suffocatingly fast as he walked to them, studying them.

The little white disk on one read: City 91211; that of the other was blank. The blank one was probably a house telephone, the other *might* be connected with the City exchange, not to anywhere in this building. He felt icy as he touched it.

He lifted the receiver and dialled his own number.

Brrrr-brrrr. Brrrr-brrrr.

It seemed to go on for a long time.

Then Jolly answered.

.   .   .   .   .

Now Jolly knew, and would give the police this number—speaking to Grice. Grice would hold his hand until the evening. The fate of Old Harry was sealed, but . . .

What of Anne?

And himself?

.   .   .   .   .

He looked round the bedroom. The silks and satins on the bed were expensive and luxurious, the room had a feminine touch. There were no windows, but, like his own room, this was air-conditioned. The furniture was of period walnut; there were some almost priceless ornaments, silver and gold and bejewelled. Was it a man's room?

He went to the wardrobe.

Yes, there were only men's clothes.

Was there time to search more thoroughly?

No—he had stayed too long already.

He went to the door. He had not been in the room for five minutes, and had not heard a sound outside. His guard hadn't returned, therefore there was no danger. But he switched off the light and opened the door an inch and peered out, before stepping into the passage.

As he did so a man spoke.

CHAPTER XXII

THE LAST MEETING

THE voice came from the end of the passage, and Rollison heard footsteps. He knew that a door had opened and that two men were coming towards him. He backed into the bedroom, leaving the door ajar.

If the men came here, or if they went to his room, all was over.

They turned into the passage, no longer talking. He thought he recognized Baxter's footsteps, but not Old Harry's. The men were so near that he could hear their clothes rustling, the squeak of a shoe, one man breathing asthmatically.

They stopped immediately outside the door.

Rollison stood close to the wall, gauging the chances of a desperate throw. They would come straight in, without looking right and left. If he stood close to the wall he might have a chance to slip out unseen. Then he would have to find his way through the house. First he would need a weapon.

The door didn't move, but there was a click, the familiar sound of a key turning.

The men had gone into the opposite room!

Rollison waited for a few breathless seconds, then slipped into the passage, closed the door and went back to his room. He lit a cigarette with hands which were rather unsteady; from now on the strain of waiting would be almost unbearable. It was difficult to believe that he had achieved so much, to realize that the affair was now very near its climax.

It wasn't yet noon.

By seven or eight o'clock that night Old Harry should be a prisoner, all his 'executives' with him, and——

Anne?

No point in thinking about her, or about himself. Unless he stayed, the meeting would not take place. He had to keep reminding himself of that. As it was, Old Harry might have taken precautions against an emergency.

Seven or eight hours.

. . . . .

Grice replaced the receiver, sat back in his chair, and smiled very widely. A chief inspector who looked in was so taken aback that he gaped. Grice waved him away, and the C.I. went out, shaking his head. After a while, Grice stretched forward for the telephone, and spoke to a superintendent of the City police. He wanted to know the subscriber to the telephone number City 91211.

Within ten minutes, the City man was on the line again.

"It's a man named Harriman," he said, "an ex-directory subscriber with an address in Raffety Lane——"

"Raffety *House*?" exclaimed Grice.

"No, King's Chambers—just a minute, I'll look at the map again," said the City man. "Ah, you weren't far out, it's next door to Raffety House. Is that what you wanted?"

"Just right," said Grice softly. "And you'll have a call soon, to get ready for a raid tonight."

"Anything big?" asked the City man.

Grice chuckled. "You'll see," he said, and then rang off.

He hurried out of the office, looking very youthful and with a spring in his step, until he reached the Assistant Commissioner's office. He knew that the A.C. was still deeply suspicious of Rollison, and that the story in the *Morning Echo* had heightened those suspicions.

He went in and talked earnestly to an astonished brown moustache.

. . . . .

Jolly and Armitage were among the people who watched Raffety House and King's Chambers from four o'clock that afternoon—although the police had been at hand within half an hour of the address being discovered. At five o'clock there was an exodus from both buildings. Pale-faced junior clerks and office boys, typists, messenger boys, telephonists, a few elderly clerks as well, streamed away from the two buildings which were adjacent. Each had two entrances—a main one in the Lane, a back one in an alley. The alley was closely watched; two or three men, better dressed than those who had left by the front entrances, were seen to come out, and these were followed but not questioned by the police. All of them returned before six o'clock, by which time there was hardly an office in either building with lights on, as far as the police, Jolly and Armitage could see.

At six-fifteen three men drove to the alley and, parking their cars at one end, walked briskly to the back entrance of Raffety House and went in.

There followed a lull for some fifteen minutes. Nothing happened, no one stirred. The police were watching from doorways, the windows of office buildings near by and every point of vantage, but few of them could be seen. Armitage, in a small office right opposite the front entrance of King's Chambers, tossed a cigarette into a littered fire-place, and exclaimed:

"How do we know when this precious meeting starts, Jolly? How can we be sure that the police will raid at the right time?"

"We don't know," said Jolly, "but every man who leaves either building now will walk into the hands of the police."

"And we've just got to wait? I can't stand it!"

Jolly looked at him coldly.

"Mr. Rollison has waited for a long time," he said.

.   .   .   .   .

Rollison was sent for just after half past six, and, led by Baxter and another man, walked along the narrow passage, past Anne's room, up a short flight of stairs, then along

another passage, until he reached the hall of an office building. He recognized the hall, in spite of the poor light; he
was at Raffety House, where he had been shanghaied and
from whence he had been taken away. He even caught a
glimpse of the notice board which announced: *Harry Webb
& Co.* Then he was taken up one more flight of stairs. A
dim light burned on this landing, and a door was ajar.
Baxter pushed it open and led Rollison inside.

It was a large room—larger than he had thought there
would be at this building. And he quickly saw the explanation—this room was in two different buildings. A partition
wall, which looked solid enough, was folded back in two
halves, at the sides. There was room for forty or fifty
people here—and the room was crowded with men.

They were sitting in rows, and there was a gangway at
either side but not in the middle. In all, there were three
doors, two at one end of the room, one at the other. The
air was thick with tobacco smoke.

There wasn't a woman present.

Rollison looked blankly above their heads, although they
all stared at him. He recognized a solicitor who had a first-
class reputation; a business man who was reputed to be
very wealthy, and whose Mayfair parties were famous.
There were others he knew: a member of the Stock Exchange whose reputation was beyond reproach, an eminent
Wimpole Street physician—and all these were Old Harry's
one-time victims and present associates.

The difference between this gathering and that at the
warehouse was remarkable. There the well-dressed men
had been noticeable because they were so few. Here, one or
two were untidily dressed, but it might have been any
gathering of business and professional men. They were
sitting on upright chairs which were placed in front of a
long, narrow desk, behind which were several chairs. On
the desk was a glass of water, a blotting-pad and an
inkstand; it was just as if this were a meeting of share-
holders.

And every man stared at Rollison, who was led along by the wall to the desk.

Baxter pushed a chair forward.

"Siddown," he said.

Rollison lowered himself cautiously.

Just a little more patience.

There was a stir when a door behind the desk opened, for Old Harry came in.

Rollison did not look towards him, although everyone else did. But out of the corner of his eye he saw the now familiar black beard and the flowing locks, the cold blue eyes, the neat, trim figure. Old Harry lifted his hand in greeting, and came and sat down in the chair next to Rollison—as if he were chairman of the meeting. He put a brief-case in front of him.

The doors were closed.

"Now, gentlemen," said Old Harry, "I don't think to-night's business need take very long. Most of you have been keeping in touch with events through the newspapers, and you know how successful our venture is proving. And—" he gave his little, deceptively friendly chuckle—"and you know that business is picking up. That is thanks to Rollison here, but mostly to my own long-sightedness, as I'm sure you will all agree. We are launched safely. Every aspect of the business is now properly covered; we have experts in every field. During the period of preparation we have all worked from these offices under the supervision of my good friend, Harry Webb, but soon we shall begin to disperse. Dispersal is necessary and wise, because now and again the police may have a limited success. So this will be our final meeting here."

A man said, "And time, too."

"In *good* time," said Old Harry, looking at the interrupter coldly. "Now, you are all familiar with the situation; you all know that there has been a great deal of talk about me— as Old Harry, not Mr. Harriman!—and that the police are very anxious to find me. It seems to me that the perfect climax to this period of preparation will be if they *succeed.*"

There was a noticeable stiffening among the audience.

Old Harry chuckled.

"Yes, I'm sure you see that. The police will believe that if they catch Old Harry our plans for organized crime will fail. It will be much better if they think it has failed; they will slacken their efforts, give us good time to settle down nicely. But, of course, they won't catch *me*—only a man whom they believe to be Old Harry."

No one spoke; there was tense silence.

"And I have been preparing carefully for this moment," said Old Harry. "You see, the man who has most influence in the East End of London is our friend Rollison. Let's face that. And I don't really trust him. He has been very acquiescent and helpful, but I have no doubt that he envisages the time when he will be able to turn the tables. I once suggested to him that he would be on a good thing if he aligned himself with us, but he is a wealthy man with ideals—ideals!" repeated Old Harry, and laughed as if that were a wonderful joke. "I just don't believe that he would ever become one of us. And so I spread the rumour, very stealthily, that he was none other than—Old Harry himself!"

A gasp; a man laughed; Baxter guffawed.

Rollison sat upright and very still.

"I promised him that he would regain his sight," went on Old Harry. "He will, very soon now. But the first thing he will look at is a police-cell, perhaps even the face of his erstwhile friend, Superintendent Grice. Because"—he tapped the brief-case—"here are papers which will prove to the satisfaction of any court of law that Rollison *is* Old Harry. Some of the preparations, some of the details of crimes recently committed, details of how the stolen goods have been disposed of, are in here. What is more, I have put in detailed information about the arrangements which Rollison himself made for the Brayling affair, when that

poor maidservant was murdered. There will be no doubt
in the minds of the police and of the judge and jury when he
stands his trial, because he was out that night—looking for
me! Weren't you, Rollison?"

Rollison turned his eyes towards him, narrowed as if he
still could not see.

Baxter guffawed again.

"I shall take Rollison to a small office not far from here,
where these papers will be planted," went on Old Harry.
"And the the police will be informed of his whereabouts.
They will detain him, search the office, and—well, tomorrow's headlines will read rather differently from this
morning's. May I make a guess at them? 'The Toff *is* Old
Harry!' Oh, I shall see that the Press is informed in good
time; they will be near the office, too."

He paused.

The man who had interrupted before shifted in his seat,
and called out:

"But Rollison will tell the police about——"

"Oh, come, my friend," said Old Harry. "Rollison
can't name one of us, even though he may know some,
because he can't see. And the story will be so extravagant,
so absurd, that no one will believe it. I have already heard
from a good friend that there are police suspicions about
him; they suspect that this story which he circulated about
Old Harry and the gathering of crooks is just a cover to
save himself. This deep-laid plot *cannot* fail. Rollison
himself, by his secretiveness when he first started to work
against me, has contributed to his *own* undoing." He
turned and looked straight at Rollison. "Well, my friend—
isn't it clever?"

Rollison growled, "You—*swine!*"

"Oh, of course, you are distressed," said Old Harry.
"But the day had to come when you met your Waterloo.
It is here! Now——"

He stopped abruptly, for a door at the end of the room
burst open. Two or three men on guard swung round to-

wards it, and momentarily hid the doorway from Rollison's sight. Men jumped up in alarm, even Old Harry stared with some dismay—and then he relaxed.

Rollison saw *Anne*.

She managed to push the guard away and to come running towards the desk, crying:

"You can't do it! I won't let it happen!"

CHAPTER XXIII

OLD HARRY

HER eyes were wild with alarm and horror, her hair streamed back from her head. She tripped over a man's foot, steadied herself, and then came forward. Baxter jumped towards her—but he stopped suddenly, for Anne snatched something from the front of her white blouse.

She held a gun.

A man shouted, "Watch her!"

But Baxter backed away.

Anne drew near the desk, and the gun pointed at Old Harry.

She cried: "I'll kill you, I'll make sure *you* never profit from it! And to think that *you*, of all people——"

One of the guards at the far end of the room tossed something towards her. Only Rollison and one or two at this end of the room noticed it curling through the air. It hit the wall with a thud—it was a heavy stick—and Anne dodged. As she did so, Baxter leapt forward and snatched at her wrist. She tried to free herself, but Baxter struck her, knocked her against the wall, and wrested the gun away.

"That's fixed you," he said, and glanced round at Old Harry for approbation. "She can't do no more harm, Boss."

Old Harry took an automatic from his pocket and said softly:

"Can't she, Baxter? I'm afraid she can. I have always feared that she would be difficult, that she would not accept the inevitable, and live in the luxury we could provide. She has a conscience—like Rollison. Take her away. You know what to do."

"Oke," said Baxter.

Anne cried: "You'll never get away with it! The police will catch you, all of you!" She turned to Rollison. "Don't let them do it, don't let them!"

"Shut your trap," growled Baxter, and pushed her back towards the end door. She half-turned and tried to speak again, but another man thrust his hand over her mouth.

Not a man stirred, except Old Harry, who put his gun on the desk in front of him.

She was near the door when Rollison leaned forward and took the gun from under Old Harry's nose. He pushed his chair back, stood against the wall, and fired twice into the ceiling. He moved quickly and without fuss. Plaster fell in a little shower; men jumped to their feet. Baxter released Anne and swung round. Rollison fired again; the bullet caught Baxter in the shoulder; a gun dropped from his hand. Anne broke loose and turned.

"Keep still, Anne," said Rollison, and his quiet voice sounded clearly through the room. "And you keep still, Harry," he ordered, as Old Harry began to rise. He stretched out his hand and pushed the man back in his chair. "I don't mind who makes the first false move," Rollison added, "but whoever it is will get hurt. I——"

He broke off.

A thudding sound came from outside—heavy bangs on a door. Next there was a crash of breaking glass. Old Harry tried to get up again; one of the guards put up his hand to his pocket.

"Careful," Rollison said, and the man took his hand away, empty.

Another crash, a pause—and then running footsteps.

"Go and tell them where we are, Anne," said Rollison. "Don't worry, they're the police. They must have heard the shooting."

.   .   .   .   .

George Armitage and Jolly were with Grice and the police. In the wild confusion which followed Armitage took Anne in his arms and hugged her as if she were his very existence. Plain-clothes men and police covered each entrance. Half a dozen of Old Harry's men broke out of the room but were caught before they left the premises. And through it all Old Harry sat like a stone figure.

When the confusion was over, and trapped men stared at the desk and the men there, Grice came to the desk.

"Well, Rolly."

"I think it's a fair cop," said Rollison mildly.

Grice chuckled.

"Of the Toff or Old Harry?" He turned round, looked at the bearded man, and stretched out his hand.

"Oh, no, that's my privilege," said Rollison.

Old Harry did not even struggle.

The beard came off without much trouble—far more easily than it would have come from a clean-shaven face. There was a white beard beneath it. And the wig came off, to reveal a nearly bald pate.

Grice exclaimed, "That's Richard Grey!"

"Anne's uncle," murmured Rollison. "Poor Anne."

George Armitage still had his arms round Anne.

.   .   .   .   .

Snub sat up in bed, smoking, eager-eyed. Rollison sat by his side, talking, telling the whole story, answering questions. Now and again Snub rubbed his hands together, and once, in an excess of joy, he clapped them loudly. A nurse looked in, but Snub waved her away. That story took some telling, for Snub was thirsty for details, but at last even his flow of questions dried up, and Rollison chuckled.

"Can't you think of any more, Snub?"

"Plenty more tomorrow," said Snub. "My sainted Aunt Agatha, what a show! And you always thought it was something fantastically big, didn't you?"

"It had all the signs," said Rollison.

"The damned fool—to get them all together like that!"

"But he believed it was quite safe," said Rollison, "especially as most of his executives were actually on the premises. They didn't have to come to the meeting from outside, and thus perhaps arouse police suspicions. Old Harry banked everything on my being blind, knew nothing about that last telephone call."

"Your eyes *are* all right, aren't they?" asked Snub anxiously.

"Oh yes—sight's a bit dim for long distances, but that will right itself. I was injected with mydriatic, which dilates the pupils so much with its atropine content that you can't see clearly. The bump over the head made the blindness complete for a few days. The stuff was pumped in by one of the doctors on Old Harry's staff, who was taken ill afterwards, and couldn't give me a second dose to be sure the blindness remained. Old Harry just judged my condition by the obvious indications, and fell for the bluff. Well, they're all at Brixton now, under remand. The court was a sight this morning. They put 'em all together in the public gallery for the charge, and Grice got a fourteen-day remand on them all. Old Harry was charged separately."

"Brilliant man just gone wrong," remarked Snub.

"That's it," agreed Rollison. "Suffering from a grievance, partly real, partly imaginary. We'll never stop crime until we get all social conditions right, but that's another story. Well, I'd better——"

"Just a minute!" exclaimed Snub. "I've thought of another one. Why did they go after George?"

"What a question to forget!" scoffed Rollison. "It is really very simple. One day when George was in Harry Webb's office—Webb was in the country, the police have him now—he saw old Harry as he really was—Richard Grey. So they had to get George one way or another, and we know the way they chose. Baxter went to pieces on the night of that job. He forgot something, and actually visited Old Harry at the Muswell Hill house. You were right, the Lagonda was parked there. Then they sent the little chap after George——"

"What about those blanks?" demanded Snub.

Rollison said slowly:

"Philip Rowse put them in the gun. He knew that the man was coming to kill George, and—well, there were limits to how far Philip Rowse would go. I think that will be in his favour; he'll probably get a lighter sentence than most. Rowse was the chief selling agent for jewels, of course, and used his beauteous damsels to dispose of them, he wasn't just the roué that George imagined. Oh, it's been an ugly business," Rollison went on. "Anne, suspicious and worried because of her uncle's visitors, his story that he was being blackmailed, which nearly put us off the right scent—but that hardly matters now. He wanted to keep her out of it, but she was far too persistent. In the end, he would have killed her."

"Not a hope," said Snub.

"I tell you——"

"Not a hope, with you around," declared Snub.

Rollison laughed as he stood up.

"I won't argue. Anyhow, I think she and George will make a match of it. No money worries now, and the police won't charge George, who was acting under duress. Anne will keep him steady."

"Lucky George," said Snub. "But why didn't they kill him when they had him?"

"That's very easy to answer," said Rollison. "He had become a wealthy man—they were going to get his money before finishing him off."

"Nice show altogether," said Snub.

Rollison left the nursing home and walked towards Piccadilly and Gresham Terrace. It was strange to be at ease, not constantly on guard against making a tiny but disastrous slip. And the whole plot was smashed—the smaller criminals would not work together again, they would make their own plans, take their own desperate chances.

They would be happier.

Rollison laughed at that odd thought.

Everything took on a new meaning. Little things he had learned to take for granted showed up vividly—shop windows, scrawled chalk marks on walls, the patient, persistent newsboys, the expressions on the faces of the passing people, people who could see. He neared Gresham Terrace, and stopped abruptly.

An old man dressed in rags, with a box and a card pinned to his chest, was playing a tin whistle. The card read:

STONE BLIND

Rollison took out his wallet . . .

The blind beggar gazed blankly forward a few seconds later, clutching a handful of notes.

Rollison turned into Gresham Terrace, and the first thing he saw was an antiquated Ford standing outside 55G. Behind it was his own car; so the police had found that. He was smiling when he went upstairs—and Jolly, smiling, was at the open door.

"Hallo, Jolly!"

"Good afternoon, sir. Mr. Ebbutt——"

"Cor strike a light!" cried Ebbutt, shouldering Jolly aside, "am I glad to see yer, Mr. Ar! 'Ad a proper turn, I 'ave! You reely okay?"

"Fighting fit, Bill," said Rollison.

"That's fine—that's wonderful, Mr. Ar! Cor, wot a do! But it's all over nar. The boys was crazy to think yer'd back Old 'Arry, Mr. Ar, but it *looked* pecooliar. Tell yer wot—come aht to the gym an' 'ave a word wiv the crahd ternight, will yer? A lot of them was all ready in case yer wanted us, but I knew yer wouldn't call us if the police could do the job." He scowled. "Let 'em do the dirty work," he said, and then he became eager again. "Will yer come?"

"Of course. Half past eight all right?"

"We'll be waiting," said Bill Ebbutt.

When he had gone, Rollison and Jolly stood in the study-cum-living-room near the trophy wall. Jolly had a beatific smile, which made him look younger, and certainly proved that he was contented. His smile remained even when Rollison took from his pocket a small envelope, and from the envelope a little tuft of black hair.

"This will remind us of Old Harry," he said, and pinned it on to a small case which contained some samples of poisons used many years ago.

"We won't need reminding, sir," said Jolly. "May I suggest that you move that specimen a little to the right?"

THE END